T0086459

MOLLY'S WORLDS AND WONDERS

ROGER GRIMSON

authorHOUSE®

AuthorHouse™
1663 Liberty Drive
Bloomington, IN 47403
www.authorhouse.com
Phone: 1 (800) 839-8640

© 2017 Roger Grimson. All rights reserved.

No part of this book may be reproduced, stored in a retrieval system, or transmitted by any means without the written permission of the author.

Published by AuthorHouse 06/15/2017

ISBN: 978-1-5246-9665-8 (sc)
ISBN: 978-1-5246-9664-1 (e)

Print information available on the last page.

Any people depicted in stock imagery provided by Thinkstock are models, and such images are being used for illustrative purposes only. Certain stock imagery © Thinkstock.

This book is printed on acid-free paper.

Because of the dynamic nature of the Internet, any web addresses or links contained in this book may have changed since publication and may no longer be valid. The views expressed in this work are solely those of the author and do not necessarily reflect the views of the publisher, and the publisher hereby disclaims any responsibility for them.

Contents

This book is dedicated to my wife, Linda, for
her support, suggestions, and encouragement—
and patience—in its coming to be.

Preface

These pages describe curious life forms, other universes, beauty, magic, mysterious realms of space-time, spirituality, and more.

I previously published a story, "Molly", which received pleasing comments from readers. It describes Molly's lone arrival from a remote planet to her hidden home on a clearing in a dense forest on Earth; her physical transformations; and the knowledge she brought with her, which she shared in her developing friendships on Earth with Exi and Chel.

This book begins with some tailored adjustments of that story, now titled "Here's Molly." Then it takes off into other untold worlds of wonder and adventure when Molly moves in with her adopted Earth family—Exi and Chel's grandparents.

But Molly and friends are not the only primary characters. When Molly moves in, Grandpa and Grandma begin to deeply fathom and visit hitherto unknown mysterious realms. So the book is not only for the young. It's for those of any age who wonder about the cosmos and remarkable forms of life.

While the stories have varied plots and endings, they blend, forming a novel of a genre some would label as magical realism, or maybe as high nonsense, which, like higher mathematics, helps us with a lift of enlightenment toward our understandings of our wonderlands and forevers.

Have a good read!

Here's Molly

School was out for the summer, and Exi, Chel, and their grandparents had traveled to the coast for a few days' vacation. On the morning of their first day, the two girls were relaxing and sunning in a secluded area of the beach. The beach and ocean were bright and serene. For over an hour, they listened to the waves. The only other activity came from an occasional flock of pelicans. They had just witnessed a pelican dive straight down from about fifty yards above the water for its catch and were talking about that when Exi's phone rang, and the tranquility was over.

"Hello?" Exi inquired.

"Help me!" the other voice begged. "Would you two pretty please help me?"

Then the call disconnected, leaving Exi staring at the phone with raised eyebrows.

Chel was close enough to hear the words. "What was that all about?"

"I haven't the foggiest," Exi said. "Sounded like a girl around our age, though. But I didn't recognize her voice."

"Maybe it was all a hoax. Maybe she's a prankster."

"I don't know. She sounded pretty serious to me. She did have my number … I mean, I doubt she just dialed it randomly. Oh, and she used the phrase 'you two!' Maybe she'll call back."

"You know what? We have her number. Let's be sure to save it." Chel was curious.

The day was hot, and the girls decided that now was a good time to take a break and go to the stand for a cold drink.

The stand was attached to a small restaurant surrounded by beach dunes, picnic tables, and a couple of outdoor showers. They picked a shaded table, flopped their beach belongings on it, and carefully placed full cups of soda on the table. Chel's phone rang.

"Please, please help me, Chel."

"Whaaat?" This spooked Chel. "Who is this?"

"You don't know me, but I know who you and Exi are."

Chel sat down in front of her soda. Exi slid hers next to Chel's in order to hear the conversation.

The voice continued. "All I need is a friend. For months I have been making phone calls at random, and every once in a while, a girl who sounds about my age answers. I try to get them into a conversation, but when they find out that I want a friend and to meet, most just hang up on me. Please don't hang up on me. A few did agree to meet me. But when they first saw me, they shrieked and quickly ran away."

The voice was sweet. Chel had calmed down a little and was becoming curious again. "Why did they do that?" she cautiously asked.

"Because I'm so ugly," the voice replied.

"What do you mean?" Chel glanced at Exi and shrugged her shoulders.

"I am so ugly that no one wants to be near me," the voice cried. "I just need a friend or two. I live alone. I do everything alone. Can you two and I meet?"

Chel evaded the question. "Where do you live?"

"I live in the woods, not far from your grandpa's shop. It's the forest that's behind the park—the park that's kinda between the shop and your grandparents' home."

Chel and Exi nodded at each other in recognition.

The voice continued. "That's how I got your cell phone numbers. I found them at your grandpa's shop a few days ago."

Exi pushed her mouth to Chel's phone. "So you know Grandpa … and The Magic Shop?"

"We just exchanged a few words. I've been there a few times, and I wore disguises each time. I saw your grandma there once too."

Chel stayed focused on the forest near the park. "How can any person live there? It's a jungle—so rough and thick. There's not even a path that goes in there."

2

"That's where I live alone. Few people ever see me. There's a lot that's weird about me, other than being the ugliest thing ever. If we ever meet, I'll explain more about where I live. I don't have parents that I remember. Maybe I used to, but I can't remember. And I don't go to school, but I can read. And I do teach myself things. Maybe I did go to school for a while and then just got … lost or came here from outer space or something. But I am smart, which makes up for my ugliness to a limited extent."

"What do you do?" Exi asked. "I mean do you have a job?"

"No. I'd love to work at your grandpa's shop, but that wouldn't work out, being who I am. I don't need much money. But I make things like toys, art pieces, and practical furnishings from things I find in the forest. Then I sell them to a few stores or have them on consignment. And people do like them. They just don't like me. I wear a disguise now when I go to the stores. I'm so lonely. But I have so much to tell friends. And to learn from friends. If only I had some."

Suddenly, Exi was taken aback. Her mouth wide open, she touched Chel to get her attention and quickly mouthed, "Tell ya later." Exi had remembered a peculiar conversation she overheard about a year ago—and didn't understand—when she and Grandma were at the large craft store in town. She overheard a man who might have been the manager tell a patron who was admiring a beautiful, intricate wreath that "the girl is very talented and makes beautiful stuff, but she looks like a chaos machine from outer space. So we have her come in through the back doors and send her out of here as soon as we can, before she scares away customers. Lately, she's been wearing a disguise, but she still looks weird."

Chel asked, "What's your name?"

The voice said, "That's ugly too."

"Well, what is it?"

After a pause: "Mollyboltrightstagrut."

"What?"

"Mollyboltrightstagrut."

"What part of that is your first name?"

"That is my only name."

"What is it again?"

"Mollyboltrightstagrut."

Chel had to break it up into simpler syllables. "Molly-bolt-right-stag-rut. Is that right?"

"Yeah. Ugly, huh?"

"Can we call you Molly for short?"

"No. That's the name I came with, and I feel that I need to be called that. Can we meet, pretty please?"

Chel hesitated. "Well … I would have to talk with Exi about that." She paused and noticed Exi's contemplative expression. "Okay, I'll talk with her and call you back in a few minutes. We have your number."

"Please, please call back," Mollyboltrightstagrut begged.

"Bye now," Chel said.

Exi and Chel stared in disbelief at each other. Finally, Exi said, "Oh, what the heck. It may be interesting. Let's call her back."

Mollyboltrightstagrut answered the phone on the first ring.

"Okay, we'll meet you," Chel said.

"Oh, that is truly, truly so wonderful! I'm so happy. Can't wait, can't wait, can't wait …"

"But you'll have to," Chel interrupted. "We're at the beach and won't be back till Thursday. Tell you what. We will meet you on Friday in the park." Chel looked at Exi and received a nodding approval. "At the children's playground. One o'clock."

$$\Diamond$$

Exi and Chel waited, sitting on swing seats, pleased that no children were there in case she really did scare people. This thought had occurred to them only on their arrival at the park a few minutes earlier, but since the park was empty, they figured they really didn't need to change the meeting location.

Suddenly, they heard a screech from the wild. Then they witnessed Mollyboltrightstagrut's blazing emergence from the forest. Her arms were flapping like the wings of a flying eagle. Her legs were pumping seriously; her knees rose to her chest. At every pump, she almost doubled over. Her head bobbed like a chicken's. At varying angles, she jigged forward to meet Exi and Chel, occasionally unleashing a wide sideways hop. Halfway to the girls, she abruptly executed a cartwheel followed by an ice skater's spin before she fell down and rolled the rest of the way. She jumped up in front of them and kept jumping for a few seconds. She stretched out her arms, and her hands rapidly twitched open and shut.

"Hug me!" she chirped.

"Whoa!" the girls exclaimed in unison. They stood behind their swings, facing the most unusual-appearing "person" that they would ever face.

The first thing they noticed about her face was her incredibly large eyes. At first, their irises vibrated from side to side, almost with the speed of a plucked guitar string. Then they began swirling around like the tip of a fan blade. One rotated clockwise and the other counterclockwise. Her nose wildly puffed out and then sucked back in, like the motion of a huffing blowfish. She waved her ears as if they were her hands, evidently in a gesture that said hello. Her purple hair stood straight out, making her look like one of those cartoon characters who'd just plugged a finger into an electric outlet. Then there was her smile. It literally went from ear to ear, and the ends of her smile rapidly flapped at her earlobes.

She began frantically running in place, looking upward again and erratically flailing her arms. "Please don't run away," she begged. "Oh, but the two of you are so beautiful. I wish, I wish!"

Chel declared, "Mollyboltrightstagrut, you really aren't ugly. You're just extremely peculiar."

"What?" Mollyboltrightstagrut was instantly motionless. "I'm not ugly? Did I hear that right? Oh!" Then she began hopping around in circles, looking up into the sky while thrusting her arms upward.

Exi agreed with Chel. "You're just … unusual. Your appearance, that is. And your movements."

"My movements?" She clasped her hands and placed them under her chin. "Oh, I see. I'm just excited, but I'll calm down. You did not run away, and you did not call me ugly." She rapidly pumped up and down on her toes a few times. Then she stood still. She extended her right hand while shyly looking down. Exi and Chel extended theirs, and they shook hands.

"Tells us about yourself," Exi said. "Where do you come from?"

Mollyboltrightstagrut sat down on the ground facing Exi and Chel, who sat back down on the swing seats. "That's one of my problems," she said. "I am working on that." The two sisters were staring at her in bewilderment. Her eyeballs were now bobbing up and down, but as one went up, the other went down. "I think maybe from outer … I had to leave my … home. The first thing I clearly remember was waking up in this little house back there in the forest, about two years ago. Before that, I have very few memories. I'll tell you more about that when we become friends."

Exi interrupted. "Are you saying there is a house back in that jungle of crowded trees and brambles?"

"Yes. With two large rooms, one about the size of a large master bedroom, and the other larger than most living rooms. A small house but neat. I like it. But there is something extremely extraordinary about it. I'm almost afraid to tell you because not only will you think I'm ugly, but you will think I'm a liar as well."

"We already agreed that 'ugly' is not the right word. You're not ugly," Chel said. "So go on with your lie." Chel was joking now, and she gave a short laugh. Then she suddenly felt embarrassed for giving the appearance of being too familiar with someone so odd whom she had just met, even though she was enjoying the conversation.

But to her surprise, both Exi and Mollyboltrightstagrut gave a chuckle.

"Okay, I'll tell you about the house. But don't run away."

"We promise," Exi said, speaking for her sister as well.

"It's invisible."

"No way!" Chel exclaimed. "How can anything be invisible?"

"Do you mean disguised?" Exi asked.

"Invisible from the outside, if the windows and front door are closed. Not from the inside. Inside, I can see the walls and things. I can look out through the windows. But from the outside, the house can't be seen. If a window or the door is open, then from outside you can see that part of the inside. And what a weird sight that is! The animals can't see it. But they know by adverse experience that it's there, and they stay away.

"I remember waking up in one of the rooms, the bedroom—the other room I call the 'everything room'—and not knowing where I was nor where I came from. But over the past two years, my memory of the past has been returning. Except for me, there was not another thing in the house other than things that were attached. No furniture, no toiletries ... although there is a small bathroom in the bedroom."

She paused for a moment, thinking, and then she continued. "Oh right! No, nothing. Not even clothes. Later I made some clothes from leaves and acorns ... and from thistles and such. I discovered that I needed clothes after I ventured a little farther out of the area for the first time one day and saw clothes on people. They saw me too, and became frightened. That's when I learned the importance of being careful: how to hide and how to disguise myself. Another story. Again I'm getting ahead of ..."

"So what did you do when you first woke up in this invisible house?" Chel asked.

"Okay, the first thing I did was just look around. I walked around, cautiously, in utter confusion. I studied the walls, the floors, the ceiling, and the corners. I looked through all the windows. I saw a small, bright green yard surrounding the house, and beyond that I saw trees and roots and branches and thick bushes everywhere. I went to the door and eased it open, peeking out as I did so. I haven't a clue how in the world a beautiful yellow rose, not to mention the green yard, can grow in a place so dominated by such dense foliage. But there it was, welcoming me to this world.

"I carefully stepped outside and looked around. That's when I turned and realized I could not see the house. Instantly I flailed around, immediately hit the door, and dashed back to safety. But through a side window of the door, I stared for a while at the rose. I wish I were a rose."

"Tell us about the rooms," Exi requested.

"As I've said, nice things are attached in the rooms—attached to the walls and floors and ceilings. There is a constant flow of fresh water from a small waterfall in the everything room. I can put a glass in it for cool water to drink. I can adjust the temperature and take a shower in it. I can turn it on and off. My water is supplied by a well, and my electricity is supplied by a generator outside in the back. There is beautiful music all around and controls on a wall for selections and volume. There's a built-in stove and refrigerator. A built-in TV and radio. Let's see. There are shelves, attractive ceiling lights, curtains, blinds, a few cabinets. Modern, good quality. Now that I have made furniture, utensils, and stuff, it's comfortable there."

These descriptions spurred her to reflect back. "It was difficult at first. I didn't know much. I got my first meals from garbage cans. I knew I needed tools, so I kept my eyes open for them. I eventually scrounged some up, although my first creations for sale were made from vines and small branches, and my first tools for those were my hands and teeth—and sometimes some spit. At first these were mainly baskets and wreaths. Later I made more sophisticated items."

Then she got back on track. "Oh … the house … There is one extraordinary thing in my little house. But you will have to see it to understand it."

"What is it?" Exi asked.

"It's a huge telescope. It's in the center of the everything room, and it extends through the cathedral ceiling to way beyond the treetops. At twice the height of the tallest tree, it has built-in mechanisms that allow me to rotate it and aim it in any direction from the control panel so I can see throughout the cosmos. You won't believe this, but I can extend the telescope so far out and bend it so much, all from the control panel, that I can view the depths of the cosmos from the other side of the world. But you will have to look into it to fully appreciate its applications."

"What do you mean? What do you see?" Chel asked.

Mollyboltrightstagrut shrugged her shoulders. "You'll have to see for yourselves. Of course, I'll be there to explain certain things."

Exi and Chel looked at each other, and Exi responded. "It sounds interesting, but I don't know. I'll talk with Chel about it. And maybe with my parents and grandparents."

"I completely understand," Mollyboltrightstagrut said. "Just please don't tell anyone where my house is located."

Exi made an observation. "Despite all these years being around here, we've never seen a telescope rising above the trees."

"It's part of my little house. It is invisible from the outside."

Exi and Chel again glanced at each other as if to say: This really can't be! Yet at the same time, they realized that they were conversing with the most unusual life-form they could ever imagine.

Mollyboltrightstagrut jumped up with her hands folded under her chin and her ears waving. "Tomorrow," she said. "Please?" However, now her eyes were more focused. Exi and Chel smiled.

The three agreed to meet at the same time, but at the edge of the forest, further from the play area, in case children—or adults—were around. Exi and Chel watched in amazement as Mollyboltrightstagrut executed a series of cartwheels, rolling off to the forest.

$$\Diamond$$

On their walk to their grandparents' home, Exi and Chel deliberated over whether or not to visit the house in the forest. "Exi, do you believe all that—that there is a house in there, number one; and number two, that it's invisible?"

"Well," Exi said, "she did come out of the forest and she went back in there. And she knows a lot about it. Yeah, I think she lives there. So she must have some kind of house."

"And what about that mysterious telescope?" Chel continued.

"Why would she make up bizarre stories if she is trying to make friends?" Exi countered. "Plus, she seems so sincere." Exi reflected on that for a few seconds. "I doubt it's a scam. What would anyone get from us—this week's allowance? Ha!"

"Yeah, I think she's sincere too. Actually, I kinda like her," Chel said. "She sure is smart ... and interesting," Exi added. I wish we could ..." Chel intercepted Exi's thoughts. "Wish her into becoming normal." They walked in silence for a minute. Then Chel turned to Exi. "Let's go!" Exi gave her a smile. "We gotta be crazy."

$$\Diamond$$

Mollyboltrightstagrut was there first. She was hiding behind some bushes at the forest's edge, and popped out at the sight of Exi and Chel approaching. This time her appearance was not so bizarre, though she rapidly raised and lowered her arms about ten times. When Exi and Chel slowed down, Mollyboltrightstagrut ran right up to them. Exi and Chel reservedly exchanged simple cheek-to-cheek greetings with her. Then they gave her a friendly once-over.

"Hi Mollyboltrightstagrut," Exi said. Exi squinted. Something was a little different about her. Now Exi stared at her directly. "You look … well … not quite as extreme."

Chel agreed. "Yeah, and you don't have as many of these seriously odd twitches and such."

"Oh, don't I wish," Mollyboltrightstagrut said. "I really wouldn't know. I don't often look into a mirror. I guess I'm just calmer today. But I want to tell you something. I thought about our conversation, and I changed my mind about something that I said. Just call me Molly for short."

"Okay," Chel said. "That makes life a little simpler." They all smiled before turning to face the forest.

"Do you dare?" Molly asked.

"Yes!" chimed the other two.

This odd forest was an area where few had ever ventured. It was more like a jungle: dark and treacherous, crammed with low branches, raised roots, vines, briars, and other impediments. Exi and Chel had come prepared. They wore protective hats, safety glasses, long-sleeved shirts, gloves, work jeans, and hiking boots. In their backpacks, they carried a sufficient supply of bottled water and some insect repellant. Molly led the way, slithering among the brambles and trees like a lizard through a familiar maze, though a bit slower than usual. The other two followed closely behind. Exi and Chel were amazed by what they saw. Sometimes they needed to step over raised ground and roots and duck under low branches. At one point they heard what they thought was the hoot of an owl, and when they looked up, they saw a great diversity of dense foliage and only small sections of the big, bright sky.

Chel called up to Molly. "You *are* going to lead us back out of this jungle, right?"

"Oh I'll think about it," Molly joked. But in an instant she excitedly announced, "Of course I will!"

Upon hearing this brief exchange in the middle of a jungle, Exi surmised that this sounded like they were all becoming better acquainted, and she smiled.

After twenty minutes of rugged travel, they came to a small clearing that dramatically contrasted with the dense forest and stopped. It looked like a vast, brightly-lit golf green with a beautiful yellow rose growing near its center. Oddly, there was no rosebush—just the rose. And Molly told them that it was always there.

"Now both of you walk over to the other side of the green and tell me what you see there," Molly commanded.

"No way!" Exi exclaimed. "And collide with something we can't see!"

"So you really do believe in the invisible house," Molly said softly with a happy smile.

"Yeah, guess we do." Exi and Chel gave each other a quick glance. Then they caught Molly's smile, and they both thought that it was nearly humanlike and sweet. It was not nearly as extreme as the ear-to-ear flitter that they'd witnessed the day before.

"Follow me closely," Molly said, "and stay to the left of the rose. The door is just to the left and behind the rose."

They filed toward the door. Exi and Chel felt some hesitation, but their anticipation for adventure took over. As soon as Molly passed by the rose, she stopped, extended her left arm, felt around a little, grasped something not visible, twisted it, and pushed with her arm while letting go of her grip. An awakening image emerged. It appeared at first as a long, thin, vertical line, but it widened to three feet. They stared into the everything room at the giant telescope, which was anchored soundly to the floor and ascended upward through the high cathedral ceiling. They heard the most beautiful music: a combination of new wave, light classical, and spiritual—and a presentation of several instruments, featuring the echoes of flutes, strings, a piano, and angelic soft hums. Yet there was something extra in those sounds that they could not identify—and they loved it. This was a warm, loving, and fascinating presentation of a home.

Molly stepped in and turned to face Exi and Chel. "Welcome to my home," she said. Her eyeballs rolled around a little, but she soon realized it. She blinked for a bit, and then focused them. "Come on in. I have prepared some snacks: some cheese and crackers—and iced tea."

Exi and Chel sauntered in through the doorway, stood still, and looked around. Molly closed the door to ensure they remained invisible. The room was larger than they had imagined. The décor had been masterfully created by Molly's artistic hands. Looking to the right, they discovered the gentle downward flow of water, cradled by a rocky wall, dropping into a small, clear pond. In front of the pond, not far from the telescope, they saw an attractive wood table about the size of a card table, but the top, sides, and legs were engraved with abstract images of planets, moons, and stars. Slid under the table was one chair. Turning and looking to the left toward the far corner, they saw a small refrigerator and stove. Next to these was a short counter with four drawers, and mounted on the right side of the counter was a sink. A window was centered on the wall, directly behind the telescope. The remainder of the wall, on both sides of the window, featured two beautiful floral paintings.

"Your home is so beautiful," Chel remarked.

"Make yourselves comfortable," Molly said. "My bedroom is through that door." Molly pointed to the door centered in the left wall, several feet to the left of the refrigerator. The girls wandered in that direction to take a look. The bed was the main attraction. It was almost as large as a queen-size bed. Of course, Molly had made it. It featured four enormous posts and a large headboard, and, like the table near the waterfall, it displayed intricate engravings of objects in the cosmos. The bed was a dark brown, and the engravings were inlaid with synthetic gold that Molly had obtained from the craft store. Another feature of the bedroom was on the wall opposite the headboard: a large bookcase packed with books. The girls, now curious, stepped over to examine the books. All were about the universe.

The bedroom was gorgeous, but one item normally found in bedrooms was missing from this one: a wall mirror. (A tiny hand-held mirror was hidden in a drawer.) Before they left the bedroom, they scanned it one last time to make sure they hadn't missed anything interesting since there was so much fascinating stuff in Molly's house. That's when Exi noticed a cord hanging from the ceiling, to the left of the bed as you face it. Then she noticed the faint lines outlining an attic door. She pointed to it. "What's that?" she asked Molly, who was standing in the doorway.

"Oh, that's my bedroom attic," Molly replied. "Would you like to see it?"

As the girls were unfolding the ladder, Molly flipped a switch near the bedroom door to turn on the attic light. The two sisters carefully climbed up, crawled in, and stood up. Wondrous colorful paintings of objects in the cosmos were the first things that caught their eyes. They were spread out on two walls that faced each other. However, the main feature of the attic was what was on the other two facing walls: two large bookcases containing hundreds of books. Exi and Chel were sure they knew their subject matter before they approached one of the cases. But when they got there, they saw that the subject matter was deeper than just eloquent descriptions of the cosmos. There were books about the foundations and theories of the universe: mathematics and physics books. These included books about the theory of relativity, the sun, galaxies, cosmic geometry, time, dark matter, quasars, solar eclipses, string theory, and ions, to list a few. They noticed that some books seemed to suggest the existence of things beyond their imaginations of reality: possibilities of different universes, other unknown kinds of realms, extraterrestrial existence, and celestial beings.

The center of the attic featured a beautiful coffee table and two small, comfortable sofas, each facing a wall of art. And there was good lighting by which to read.

Exi and Chel were absorbed. After ten minutes of exploration, Molly called up to them. "Have a good read. I'll meet you down here for snacks when you're ready."

Once they were back downstairs in the everything room, Exi said, "Molly, I thought you said your house had two rooms."

"It does," Molly replied. "Two rooms and an attic. But … okay. There are three rooms."

"Why do you have so much about the universe and the like?" Chel asked.

"I'm just inspired by what I see, and I'm always trying to understand everything better."

Despite all of the wonderful creations that adorned Molly's home, the telescope in the middle of the everything room remained its main feature. "Let's go to the table by the waterfall and snack on some cheese and crackers," Molly suggested. "Do you like iced tea? I'll just grab these two chairs. When we finish, we'll sit at the telescope, and I'll let each of you view some interesting things in the universe—especially one thing."

Sharp cheddar cheese on crackers and sweet iced tea hit the spot. The small talk centered on the moon and imaginative speculation on what might exist on the other side. Taking her last sip of iced tea, Chel finally asked, "What is the one thing that is so interesting?"

Molly stood up. "Let me show you. Bring your chairs." She stepped over to the telescope, and Exi and Chel followed. "This is a very special telescope. There is not another one like it on Earth. It can bring in anything in our galaxy that you want to view, and it can even focus on small details the way a microscope can." She pointed to a viewing screen the size of a large TV. "This is where you will see so much in the universe. Watch the screen and I will take you on a tour. I'm just going to conduct some operations using this control panel here … Okay. Now what do you see?"

"It's beautiful," Exi exclaimed.

"That's Saturn up close, with her many moons and her wide, bright ring of particles. Now watch this. I'm going to leave Earth's galaxy, the Milky Way, and go further out into the universe."

Exi and Chel viewed what looked like a thick disc of enraged fire with a small, pitch-black spot at its center.

"That's a black hole," Molly explained, pointing to the black spot. "It's something so dense that anything that comes near it gets sucked in and disappears. The gravity of that center point is so great that even light from its nearby sun travels to it and becomes, say, activated when it gets near the black hole, before it gets sucked in—that's the wide bright rim that you see. It even effects time in unfathomable ways, but … Anyway, our galaxy has a black hole—many galaxies do—but we are far, far from it, thank goodness."

The wide variety of fascinating entities and events in the seemingly infinite universe kept Exi and Chel spellbound for half an hour before

Chel returned to the question she originally raised during the snack. "What is it that you find so especially interesting in the universe?"

"Are you ready for this?" Molly asked. She adjusted some controls on the keyboard. "There it is!"

"What's so special about that?" Chel asked, staring at something unrecognizable on the screen.

"That's Earth," Molly said.

"No way!" Exi exclaimed, laughing as if it were a joke.

"Oh, but it is Earth," Molly retorted. "Look here." She pointed to an area on the screen. "You can see that this is the Gulf of Mexico. And look here. This is Florida. And over here is the west coast. And over here, you can recognize Long Island."

"It's too big—too tall—to be the United States," Exi said, studying the irregular land mass on the screen.

"This is not a map with colors and with boundaries drawn in," Molly said. She drew an imaginary line with her finger across the screen and then tapped the region above where she drew the line. "This is Canada. Most of the states are below this." Similarly, she drew a line indicating the border with Mexico.

A long pause passed before Exi spoke. "Can't be. We're *on* Earth, not looking at it from outer space."

"We're looking at a film, aren't we?" Chel asked. "You're tricking us, I know."

"I guess I'll just have to prove it." Molly had anticipated that proof would be required. She grasped a small lever that could be steered in any direction, and with this, she placed a tiny yellow dot on a certain location in the United States. Then, by pushing a button, she zoomed closer to the dot. The girls could see the land mass growing larger and the land's ocean boundaries disappearing. After a few seconds had passed, they saw trees. Then they recognized the green grass surrounding the invisible house and the yellow rose. But they also saw the invisible house!

"Now both of you two keep an eye on the screen. I'm going outside for a few seconds. Even when I come back in, don't take your eyes off the screen."

Molly stood up and went outside. A few seconds later she came back in and sat down near the girls at the control panel.

"We didn't see anything different," Exi said, still glued to the screen.

"Wait ten minutes. Have patience," Molly said politely. I wanted you to look at the screen so you would see that nothing was there … yet. Then when you do see something, you will understand how slow the speed of light is."

Even just one minute is a long time while peering into a still screen, and waiting with anticipation for something extraordinary to appear. But Molly was prepared. She had given each a cup of the most scrumptious sweet corn chowder. Suddenly, they saw the top of Molly's head coming out of the door. She took two steps to the rose, and Exi and Chel saw each foot and leg swing forward, while the other leg swayed back. She turned around to face the house. Then she looked upward to Exi and Chel. She extended an arm toward them and gave an exaggerated wave of her hand with a huge smile. "Hi there," she said, and the two actually heard that! Then she blew them a kiss.

"My God!" Exi exclaimed.

"What a spectacular showing!" Chel said. "But what's going on? And why did it take such a long time for the pictures, or images, to show up on the screen?"

"The speed of light," Molly answered. "We are so far away from Earth that any observation from Earth to here, all of which is carried by light, takes a while. When we are in this house, we are actually on a different planet. As soon as we step out the door we are on Earth. About hearing my voice, I have no clue. The speed of sound on Earth is much slower, and in the vacant regions of the universe, sound doesn't exist. Sound needs air to exist. But that's another matter."

"Another planet?" Exi was confused. "How can that be?"

Chel empathized with Exi's sentiment, but then she became puzzled by another thought. "Wait a minute. We also saw the top of the house. But it's invisible, right?"

Molly kind of brushed the questions away and changed the subject. "Oh, I'll explain those things later. And no, I don't have cameras and stuff hidden in trees to accomplish all this. I'm trying to make friends, not trouble. Besides, while I'm good with crafts, that type of technology is still a bit beyond me.

"But I do know who has that type of technology—specialized cameras, a complex telescope, and so on. And because I am trying to make friends, I do have to bring out the truth, in time, delicately.

"You two have experienced a lot here today. I'll walk you home … well, to the outer edge of the forest. Think about it. Come back tomorrow and I'll explain. I will explain everything to you. Please, pretty please." She winked twenty times in rapid succession with her right eye and again gave a huge, beautiful smile. "Tomorrow, please?"

"Absolutely."

"A hug, please?"

"Absolutely."

$\Diamond$

It seemed to Exi and Chel that over the brief time that they had known her, Molly was gradually losing some of her severe peculiarities. She was becoming more humanlike. Yet they had never considered her strictly nonhuman. After all, she was highly intelligent, well-spoken, she walked upright, and she smiled. This is why they were shocked when they met her at the edge of the forest the next day. She still had many irregularities, but she appeared to resemble a human girl.

"What's this?" Exi asked excitedly. "Did you use makeup?"

"No, why?" Molly asked.

"You sure look different," Exi said. "You're changing—becoming more human-looking. I mean …"

"What?" Molly replied, standing on her toes. "How's that possible? I think you just like me more, that's all. I'll have to break my rule of not looking into mirrors to see what you're talking about."

"Okay, let's go." Chel smiled with anticipation, and again they turned and faced the forest.

They made their way to the invisible door next to the yellow rose by way of the same twists and turns of the day before. Once inside the house, Molly took off to her bedroom, leaving the other two standing in her wake. A few seconds later, they heard some ecstatic shrieking, and

Molly dashed back to the everything room by way of two cartwheels and a jump. Then she stood still and covered her mouth with her hands. "Oops!" she cried. "I shouldn't have … Oh, what's happening? I do appear a bit more humanlike."

"Yes, over these past three days, we have seen subtle changes," Exi said. "It seems like you are actually becoming kind of, well … almost pretty. I would guess that it's happening right before our eyes. The question is, What's causing this?"

Oh, but did she react to the word "pretty," and with more self-restraint than demonstrated in previous reactions. She stood on her toes with her familiar pose of hands clasped under her chin and both widened eyes looking toward the cathedral ceiling. After a couple of seconds she dropped her hands and focused on Exi and Chel.

Then she spoke. "Yesterday you said, and Chel agreed"—she paused for a breath—"that my appearance and eccentricities seemed less extreme, so I gave this some thought. Let's sit at our table here by the waterfall. I have some things to disclose to you. The time is right because now you will understand. Also, just recently, I've made some new observations that I need to share with you two. First, I'll bring the snacks and iced tea."

"I smell corn chowder," Exi announced.

"I'll bring that too," the hostess replied with a wink.

"Oh, and in the meantime, use some of my books to study up on the universe," she said jokingly while skipping off to the kitchen area.

Chel and Exi looked at each other and then snuggled into their comfortable chairs at the table.

◊

"Let me begin by simply saying that there has been a genetic mix-up in the cosmos," Molly said laughingly. "I'm sorry. It's just that I'm in such a good mood today. I'll start over. Let me simply say that I don't have all the answers.

"Going back to the first day we had a conversation, when you were at the beach, do you remember me saying that maybe I came here from outer space, or something? There is no 'or something' about it. Of course I couldn't get into that then, or we wouldn't be here now, but I am from outer space."

"Oh my God!" Chel exclaimed loudly, catapulting herself upward off of her chair. Everyone immediately became quiet at this display. But Exi and Chel believed it instantly. Their reactions were more of relief than of surprise. It explained so much. Chel, now a little embarrassed, followed up with a more reserved statement, slightly louder than a whisper, while sitting back down: "I knew that."

Now the focus was on Molly. "Okay," she said, "you recall from yesterday that whenever you are in my house, you are on another planet, but as soon as you walk out the door you are back on Earth, right? And that it took ten minutes for the kiss to arrive?"

The two nodded.

"Early on—and I know so much more now—I wanted to know where I was while in the house. I did some calculations. Light travels almost six trillion miles in a year. So if something is a thousand light years from us then … Oh, never mind. Let me simply put it this way …"

"Thank you," Exi and Chel mouthed in relief.

"My home is not in another galaxy. It's not so far as all that. In fact it's in our galaxy, the Milky Way. In fact, it's even in this solar system! Otherwise you would have waited years before seeing me wave and blow you a kiss from Earth! The planet you are on is where I came from."

"Oh wow!" Chel said. "I don't …"

"The sun is the center of our solar system. Mars is the next planet farther out from Earth, and Jupiter is the next one farther out after Mars. But the kicker is that when Earth and Mars are in their closest proximity to each other by way of their orbits, it takes approximately five and a half minutes for the image of Mars to reach Earth. It's similar with Jupiter, which is farther away, but at its closest proximity to Earth, it takes almost forty-four minutes for an image from Jupiter to reach Earth. So if you are peering upward to Jupiter in that near location in the night sky, the image you see is Jupiter historically—not now, but forty-four minutes ago. Are you all following?"

Thinking heads were bobbing.

"An image of this new planet requires ten minutes to arrive as you saw yesterday when my kiss from Earth took ten minutes to reach you.

Moreover, it always requires ten minutes for an image to go from this planet to Earth, or from Earth to here."

"Oh this is getting complicated," Exi announced.

Molly recognized this and quickly responded. "I'm sorry. I'll try to keep it simple. So, simplifying a little, my planet is positioned between Mars and Jupiter. It's always the same distance from Earth, and it's a little farther out from the sun, so a little faster around the sun. Same size as Earth. Earth's shadow? No. Much older than Earth. Simple enough?"

"Yeah, I guess," Exi said. "But I have a question that's been nagging me. How can we be on a planet that is that far away from Earth, and at the same time simply walk out the front door and be on Earth?"

"It seems like a paradox, doesn't it?" Molly responded. "And there is more to it than that. I don't know all the technical details, but it has to do with the inhabitants of the planet. In a few minutes, when I describe these inhabitants, you will gain some insight into this."

Molly continued her dialogue. "The thing is, no astrophysicist, no scientist of any kind—no human—has ever detected this planet. Until me. It's not visible from Earth. I didn't know why for a long time. It's not in Earth's shadow like the moon is sometimes, and it's nothing like a black hole that absorbs light. The scientists there have figured out a way not to be seen by earthlings. Moreover, it can't be discovered using other equipment designed for detecting land mass and such. It can't even be seen by astronauts traveling near it. And it can't be hit by anything traveling toward it. But let's go to the telescope so I can show you the invisible planet."

"What?" Exi asked. "You just told us that the planet was invisible."

"It is, to earthlings on Earth. But don't forget that you're not on Earth. You are on my planet. I know, I know, it breaks fundamental laws of geometry and physics. If you are in a house, and the house is on Earth, you would think that you would be on Earth—not off on some faraway planet. But the inhabitants work with many advanced geometries. It's a radically different environment there ... I mean here. You two can see Earth because you are looking at it from a faraway planet using a super telescope, and we can see the invisible planet using reverse telescopy because we are on it."

Exi and Chel were not going to get near that one—at least not at this time.

"Is that why you know so much about Earth?" Chel asked.

"I've been studying the planet for about two years. Not a day goes by without at least peeking in. It's the only other planet in our solar system that maintains advanced life, although there is advanced life on places around some other suns in the Milky Way … and in other galaxies."

Molly paused and mentioned in a softer tone, "There is much mystery out there." Then she gathered herself and continued operating her telescope.

She did some figuring at the attached electronic, three-dimensional, curved coordinate system, and then she positioned the small yellow dot and pushed the button to bring in an image. A tiny ball appeared, and then it grew to the size of the screen. "That's it: the invisible planet," she announced. And what a sight it was. It looked like a symbol of love. It appeared as a circle with a perfectly shaped, large, deep blue heart in its center, surrounded by yellow. "The blue is one of the oceans, and the yellow is the land," she explained.

"Could we move closer? I would like to see what's on the land," Chel said.

"We will do that another time, after I've explained some things to you," Molly said. "By the way, this is why you could see the house through the telescope, Chel, when you and Exi were telescoping me while I was standing out by the rose. Through the telescope, the house was visible because you were looking at it, not from Earth, but from the other planet. The house is invisible to earthlings on Earth, as I've explained.

"Now I must tell you what this is all about. Now that my memory of the past has improved, I remembered my people telling me about Earth, and where it is, and where we were. They were preparing me for the trip to Earth. We have named this planet Friend. My people, the *friendlings*, sent me here from Friend."

"Why would they do that?" Chel asked.

Molly continued. "Not for ill-spirited reasons. Friendlings are a kind and loving people. They sent me to see if it would help me improve my looks. My people are very advanced technologically, intellectually, culturally, scientifically, and in many other ways. We have existed several billion years longer than earthlings have, so we have made so much more advancement. In fact, we existed five billion years before the sun and the solar system existed. Ten billion years ago, the friendlings moved their planet here because their original solar system was on the verge of collapse. The friendlings' super-intellectual abilities and scientific advancement permits them to develop the technology to do these seemingly impossible things. The moment there is peace on Earth, Friend will become visible, and the friendlings will join the earthlings as partners in the continuous quest for intergalactic and celestial understanding and universal peace." Molly paused, letting Exi and Chel exchange incredulous looks.

"How … advanced … are they?" Exi was almost afraid to ask.

"Let me explain by giving you a comparison. It involves the flying disk that hovered over Chicago's O'Hare Airport in 2007 and was seen by many credible people, including pilots, service people, and passengers. After twenty minutes, this craft took off upward with an incredible acceleration and put a hole in a large, thick cloud so that the observers could see the blue sky beyond the cloud. Yet radar and other surveillance equipment did not detect it. Whatever beings created this craft were advanced enough that they were able to make the craft invisible to cameras and radar, but they were not advanced enough to make it invisible to the more biologically complex human eye. The friendlings are more advanced. They made Friend invisible to the human eye—and they made my house invisible too. There! You see?"

Chel needed more information to satisfy her curiosity. "How in the world would coming to Earth help you to improve your looks?"

"They sent me here because I was so vastly different-looking that it was causing problems with many friendlings. These wonderful people are very different in appearance from earthlings. They're about the same size as humans, but their features are much different. Their heads are round, about the size of a basketball, with three circular eyes. Light always beams out of their eyes. Their mouths are thin but long and so wide that they extend out beyond their faces. A string of twenty or so bottom teeth protrude outward and are always visible. When they smile, the ends of their mouths bend downward. Their necks are thick and short, with Adam's apples that stick way out and are shaped like thorns, followed immediately by shoulders that droop drastically down. Their arms are about half the size of human arms, and each hand has only four fingers. Their chests and stomachs are shaped like two-drawer file cabinets. And they don't have knees, so their gait is odd by human standards. Ten toes are on each foot. Those are just a few of the differences.

Of course, they see each other as normal. They are great beings, just … different-looking. And I scare them. So when they look at me, it's as if …okay … as if you humans suddenly saw a dust mite the same size as you. Or a silver fish, or a bacterium, or a black widow spider, or a rattlesnake … except your size. Not just a wacky, spiraled-out, almost girl. Know what I mean?"

Thinking heads were still bobbing. "Oh yeah. Now that is really ugly," one head said.

"My approaching another friendling produces the same reaction as you would experience if an open-mouthed rhinoceros with dinosaur fangs approached you. So the friendlings had to do something."

"But Molly, you still haven't answered my question about coming to Earth," Chel remarked.

"I'm getting to that. The friendlings concluded that out of all the advanced life forms that they know of, humans are the closet to resembling ugly me. Now listen very carefully with an open mind to what I have to say next. There is much more variety, or variability, or differences … I'm trying to find the best word … *huge differences* will do. There are huge differences in appearance among the folks on Friend. Friendlings can change and improve their appearance under certain circumstances, within limits. It's odd. If one is considered not good-looking, or even ugly, by another, and the other loves or likes the personality of the ugly one, then the ugly one will notice an improvement in his or her own appearance. The reason for this—and I think it's because of the advanced state among the friendlings—is that character comes first. Physical appearance is secondary. Generally, it's just the opposite on Earth."

Molly caught the quizzical looks on the girls' faces and said, "Sorry. Simple, simple!"

Exi felt a strong need to understand this. "Character comes before appearance in attraction? Sorry, Molly, I don't understand."

"Okay, let me explain it this way. On Earth, personal appearance is the first thing in general attraction. Character comes later. And the character of a person is often obscured by the attraction the one looking sees. On Friend, character is the first thing experienced in love and in friendship. That is, love and friendship are first based on character, and looks are secondary. Inner beauty surfaces before outer beauty ..."

Exi interrupted. "So ... do you mean that on Friend, appearance is not nearly as much noticed as character when one is getting to know another? Let me see ... If, say, Bill is attracted to Ann because of her good character, and Ann isn't good-looking, then Ann's appearance will improve. Is that what you mean?"

Molly smiled. "Oh, you and your sister are so bright! You ask such great questions. Yes, that is a good way of putting it. Ann's appearance will improve up to the level of her character.

"On Earth you may wish a person's character to change after the physical attraction for that person takes hold. But good luck. On Friend, it's the opposite. You may want the physical appearance to change after the love or friendship with a desirable character or personality is developing. And that is much easier. It comes about by the wishing, or the hoping, by the one who is attracted to the ugly one's character. This came about among friendlings as we have developed ourselves over time on Friend. Simple enough?"

"Yes?" The girls answered hesitantly.

Chel added, "Character or personality, the second stage on Earth, can't change. But appearance, the second stage on Friend, can change."

"That's right." Molly said. "Look at it this way. Suppose you have a friend, and one of the reasons that you like her is due to certain aspects of her character or personality, in addition to common interests and so on. But suppose she's ugly, and she wishes that she could be attractive. Further, suppose you had a way to make that happen, say by a superior ability to wish. Wouldn't you do that for her?"

"Oh yes!"

"Okay, good. But like all things, as I alluded to, there are a couple of limitations. The first—and I mentioned this a minute ago—is that your physical beauty can develop only to the extent of your inner beauty, your character. Even though we are advanced, we are still only friendlings.

"The other limitation is this: If someone is *extremely* ugly, I mean ugly enough to cause fear as I did to them—like a two-hundred-pound spider with fangs would do to most humans—then the progression toward beauty won't happen."

Molly paused, and Chel took over. "So they sent you to Earth with the idea that you would not appear so extremely ugly to humans that you would cause fear because you looked kinda humanlike. Still, some humans might like your character and become friends, and then, as your new friends would wish, you would gradually become prettier from a human perspective—and have a happy life as a human, as Exi and I hope."

"Exactly," Molly said with a tear in each beautiful eye. "And there is something else that I figured out in the last day or so. I feel my features changing as I pass by the yellow rose. And the more we get to know one another and become friends and hug, the more I feel the changes when I walk by the rose. And I think the rose has some effect even when I'm in the house. I never knew the purpose of its existence. The friendlings must have planted it here when they built my house. Let's step out the door to Earth and be by the rose."

The three went outside onto the sun-brightened green. Molly looked down at the rose, and then she looked up, and with both hands, she wildly blew a kiss into the sky. She felt the kiss return, one on each cheek ... and then she realized that Exi and Chel had given them to her.

"Molly, you are beautiful!" Chel declared.

Exi agreed. "You have the grace of an angel."

"It was the hugs, friendship, the best wishes, the good character, and the supportive magic of the yellow rose," Molly said.

Exi and Chel were stirred. They looked at each other, and in the presence of Molly's smile, the two embraced in a huge hug. And when they parted, each holding both hands of the other and bending slightly back for a good look at the other, a pose sometimes observed in reunions of long-parted friends, each noted that her sister was a bit more beautiful than before.

Let Go

Molly got her wish. The Magic Shop was Molly's first place of employment since she became presentable for inclusion among the lives of humans. And she loved it. She was available and wanted an earthly job. So thanks to her new friends' testimony, Grandpa was pleased to hire her as the part-time helper he needed in the shop. Moreover, he somehow acquired a vexing suspicion that she may somehow contribute to the magical allure of the shop.

Grandpa and Grandma had yet to fully understand Molly's background. They welcomed the likeable earthling, though they received occasional impressions that "elsewhere" may somehow be involved. Exi and Chel were astute enough to lay low on key details for a while, revealing tidbits of info as time went on. Besides, Grandpa and Grandma assumed the obvious: that she had been well cared for. She was a pleasantly welcomed newcomer.

Molly began much of her social development during her employment at The Magic Shop. This was a popular shop. The items for sale there included more than devices for magic shows and the like. The tables and shelves stocked many unusual or foreign gift items and curious toys for all ages. With Grandpa's coaching, she quickly learned to imaginatively demonstrate and describe items to shoppers. Exi and Chel brought their parents to the shop to introduce them to Molly soon after her employment, and after Grandma's cheerful comments about the new girl there.

Molly loved to visit Exi and Chel at their grandparents' home, which was within walking distance of the shop and from her home in the forest. She especially liked to spend time in the Rainbow Room, where she enjoyed its beauty and comfort, and where she felt her conversations were somehow enriched. The Rainbow Room is what they called the screened-in porch on the left side of the house as you face it. It contains comfortable furnishings and is regularly adorned with cheerful floral arrangements.

This is where Grandma spent much of her time reading, crocheting, or just socializing with friends and family. Also, it's where the first convincing sign of Molly's otherworldly persona was witnessed— two months after her friendship with the family began. It was in the morning. Grandma was joined by Chel and their sweet little spaniel puppy, Sparkles. Molly was expected to visit later. However, her presence was felt by Chel early on.

Chel had been reading comfortably, with Sparkles cuddled up to her on the love seat, when she calmly looked upward, sensing something stirring around the ceiling. Suddenly, her eyes widened, and she abruptly stood up. She saw an elusive presence while fixating on the corner of the ceiling near the door to the living room. Sparkles was eyeing the area too. Chel murmured, "Molly?"

Then she turned to Grandma, who witnessed this puzzling behavior. "I just felt something weird, Grandma. Not bad weird, just … a little strange."

"What do you mean, Chel?" Grandma asked. "You're not coming down with something, I hope."

"Oh no, nothing like that. I just got a little mixed up about something, I guess. I'm okay."

"Well, let me know if it happens again. And why did you call out for Molly?"

"I really don't know." She felt Grandma's five-second stare.

Grandma returned to her crocheting, and Chel sat down and picked up her book. But she and Sparkles studied the ceiling quizzically.

"Ooh," Chel whispered loudly a few minutes later. "It's happening again."

Again she looked up, and this time she walked over and peeked into the living room. "Molly?" She turned around and again faced Grandma. "What happens is that I get this strong feeling that Molly's somewhere out here in the Rainbow Room, near the living room. But she's supposed to be at the shop with Exi, helping Grandpa. At least she's not here. It starts like some kind of … confusion, and it builds up to a sense of her being here. It's like I saw her image floating, and I could sorta see through her."

Grandma intervened. "Come on, let's go inside. Lie down on the sofa and rest while I go fix lunch."

While Grandma was in the kitchen and Chel was reclining in a state of bewilderment, the front door flew open and Exi flew in, gasping like a fish out of water. "You'll never believe what just happened at the shop! … Hello!" Then she paused for more air, reaching down for Sparkles's leaps.

"It's Molly!" Exi continued in short breaths as she straightened up. "She completely disappeared! Twice! Each time for about half a minute before coming back!"

"Hold on, Exi," Grandma said as she paused and turned toward Chel. Then she faced Exi again. "Catch your breath and tell us about it."

"Okay. Where do I start? Grandpa received this … it's called a 'torus section.'"

"A what?" Chel interrupted. "What is that?"

"I really don't know what the word means, but it's like a large, silver cylinder, or pipe. I guess it's about ten feet long and big enough around that you can crawl through it. But it's very light. Oh, and it's slightly curved, but you can barely notice that."

Grandma and Chel did not respond. They simply continued staring at Exi.

"Okay, a large silver pipe, curved a little. You'll understand when you see it."

Grandma made her first inquiry. "You say Grandpa received this so-called torus section. What for? From where? Tell us more."

"He can explain it better, but he said he ordered it from a store on the outskirts of one of the largest cities in India, from Bangalore. He and Molly will be here in a few minutes. They're carrying it here now. Anyway, it appears very modern, but actually it's ancient. It belonged to an elderly man from near Bangalore who disappeared about twenty years ago and eventually was presumed dead. His family gave some of his stuff to a store to sell, including the torus section. The owner was interested in it from reading the instructions, but he could never make it work. So when Grandpa contacted him over the Internet, the guy had the instructions translated into English, and he sold it to Grandpa."

Grandma interjected, "Could never make it work? Doing what? What's it for? Let's continue talking in the kitchen."

Exi continued on the way. "You know how Grandpa likes to search out really neat things to help improve his magic shows. Well, the papers that came with it explained that if you slide certain objects—which I'll explain—through one opening hard enough to go all the way through, they would disappear going out the other end."

"Disappear? What kind of objects?" Grandma's concerns were matching her curiosity.

"Okay, here's the weird part. Grandpa said the ancient guidelines explain that the objects need to be sanctified by heavenly spirits. Something like that. Or by beings who have been so sanctified. 'Profoundly blessed' is the way Grandpa put it. Whatever!"

"Wait a minute, Exi," Chel said. "Any object that's profoundly blessed would mean something to someone. Why would someone throw such an object through a tube to make it disappear? That's like throwing a precious diamond into the garbage."

Exi explained. "In those days—and we're talking about a few thousand years ago—suppose someone wanted to see if a certain object had been blessed. They could find out by sliding it through the torus section. An object that went in and disappeared can be retrieved by a blessed one going in after it. They go to this invisible place, whatever, and come back with it. At least that's what Grandpa said the ancient instructions say. So it's not like throwing away a diamond.

"Anyway, here's what happened. Grandpa took his wand out of the closet, saying this was precious to him and was the closest thing in the shop to being blessed. He's used it in shows for years, and kissed it before and after every show. He slid it through the torus section and it came out the other end, as I expected.

"Then I, dummy me, turned to Molly and jokingly said, 'Molly you're blessed. Crawl through.'

"But then Grandpa yelled to wait. He wanted to check it out a bit more, so he very slowly crawled through first, and came out okay through the other end.

"Then it was Molly's turn. She crawled through till her head should have come out of the other end. But her head wasn't there! Through the opening where she entered, Grandpa and I saw her legs and body up to her shoulders. Oh, I still can't believe this! Then we looked in from the other end, from where she should have crawled out … just gobbledygook. This was really the inside of her neck and upper body. It was where her head and arms should have come out of the torus section. Grandpa noticed that all this stuff in there was pulsating from the heartbeat. It was crazy!

"Needless to say, Grandpa and I became terrified. We panicked. We were horsing around with something we really knew nothing about. We yelled out Molly's name, not knowing what else to do.

"Then Molly—all of her—turned around, crawled back, and climbed out where she'd climbed in."

Grandma shuddered and placed both hands on Exi's cheeks. "I find this hard to believe, but … I guess I accept it for the moment. This is frightening."

Exi continued. "Then she did it again. This time, it looked like she crawled all the way through to Lord knows where! All of her disappeared except for most of her fingers and parts of her hands, which were holding onto the rim of the torus section. The rest of her was like … nowhere."

◊

"Molly is blessed!" Grandpa loudly announced, smiling as he and Molly struggled through the front door, lugging the torus section. "This thing is light, but it's large and awkward. Wish I knew what it's made of."

Grandma came from the kitchen to the foyer followed by Exi and Chel and viewed the torus section. "Roger, this has me a bit concerned. I remember a few days ago you mentioned you had ordered something that might provide you with a great new disappearing act. But … Molly?"

"But she didn't really disappear. Look at it that way," Grandpa said while he and Molly carefully set the torus section on the floor. "She just paid a couple of short visits to another … say … place."

"What ... say ... place?" Grandma looked dubiously at Grandpa and the torus section.

Grandpa was hesitant, but he finally spoke with assurance. "Noland."

"Noland?" Grandma faced Molly. "Hi, Molly. It's good to see you. Thank God I do see you. Where'd you go?"

"I'm not sure ... Okay, Noland. There seemed to be no land there. Nothing." Then Molly's sense of humor surfaced. "Noland sounds flatter than Flatland!"

Often Grandpa doesn't grasp Molly's quips, but he continued. "Molly doesn't know much about all this yet," he declared, while waving the manual. "The information that came with the torus section was extensive, but I'm reading it all, and I'm researching more about it online. Wow, it's interesting. If only I understood more about geometry.

"Anyway, the main object is a *torus*, which is shaped like a hollow donut, or a hollow bracelet. A section out of it is called a *torus section*."

Then he paused and gazed at the torus section. "It's simple, yet ..."

Grandma remained pensive. "Let's go to the Rainbow Room and discuss Molly's ... disappearances ... over lunch. Chel, please help me in the kitchen."

Exi moved a small wicker table from the center of the Rainbow Room, and Grandpa and Molly centered the torus section on the floor. Lunch arrived, and Sparkles scampered over to join them.

Grandpa opened the discussion. "Okay. Now we're going to find out more about Molly's trips and about Noland. But first let me explain something you all should know. Evidently, a certain few people went to Noland during ancient times. They were practitioners of a religion called *Ladahala*. Not much is known about the Ladahalans. They suddenly disappeared around 700 BC. They left most of their possessions behind, including the torus section. No one knows where it came from, but the Ladahalans were familiar with it and they wrote about it. I wonder if for some reason they just went to Noland and just chose to stay there."

"This is good to know," Grandma said. "At least it begins to give me some background that I feel helps in some way, some kind of context. I'd like to know more."

"Sure. And we, in this room, are the first to explore all this within the past few thousand years."

◊

Chel then relayed her two ghostly encounters in the Rainbow Room, confirmed by Grandma's nodding. "A dramatic morning!" she said.

Chel added, "And these happenings seem to correspond to the two times Molly went to Noland. What does all this mean?"

Grandpa sat quietly through this with raised eyebrows. "That's right. This seems to jive with Molly's disappearances. Molly, what are your thoughts about this?"

"Well, the first time I went, when I reached the end of the torus section, I poked my head out and saw darkness. Heard nothing, felt nothing, smelled nothing ... *nothing!* Noland is a good name for it. I dragged myself a little more outward until my arms were reaching into Noland. Still, I couldn't see anything. I realized there was no gravity, no up and down as I could sense ... no ground. It was like part of me was floating. No, not floating. There was no air. It was like I was suspended. The upper part of me was suspended in a realm of nothingness. Whatever that means."

"No air?" Grandpa interjected. "I'm not a scientist, but I know if there's no air, there's no talking, smelling, or hearing, and such. And there would be no oxygen, so you wouldn't be able to breathe. Isn't what I'm saying correct?"

"Yes, air is the medium for our existence." Molly hesitated for a second, amazed by Grandpa's fragmented acquaintance with science. Then she tried to reason this out. "Temperature requires air, so there's no temperature. It's not absolute zero because that's a temperature. Is that right? What is no temperature?"

Molly would think more about these scientific matters later. Now she continued describing her experiences in Noland. She had to explain a link between her two experiences and Chel's. "With my head and arms hanging out and not really sensing anything, my thoughts went to Chel in the Rainbow Room."

She turned to Chel. "I thought about your joking this morning here in the Rainbow Room, you know, when I was leaving for the shop to help Grandpa experiment with this new tube he got for a disappearing act. At that time it dawned on me that maybe your joke turned out not to be a joke. Remember, you said something like, 'I hope that pipe thing gives some good magic for the shows, but don't disappear in it!'"

Molly scanned the others and continued. "As I was remembering this, all of a sudden I was there for a few seconds. Some … like … spiritual part of me was there watching you looking for me. Somehow, I think by thinking about it, I zapped back to Noland, where the opening of the torus section was. Then I crawled back to Earth, to The Magic Shop. That's what it seems like!"

"Wow!" Chel exclaimed. "What an experience. You really were here in the Rainbow Room, at least something of you was. Tell us more."

"The next time I went, I crawled almost all the way into Noland. I held on to the rim of the torus section with both hands. I imagined the Rainbow Room again, this time on purpose. Then I simply appeared there again. I was semitransparent and seemed to be floating, only it seemed like more of me was there this time.

"Again, I saw Grandma and you, and you began looking around and calling my name. As before, I didn't have much control of my movements, and I quickly zoomed back to Noland where I—my real physical me—was holding onto the torus. That's when I heard a voice.

"The voice was distant and hazy. I could barely make it out. It faintly yelled, 'Let go, let go, let go …' Then other voices around me started chanting to let go. Almost all of me was in Noland. My body felt suspended in nothingness. It seemed like if I did let go, I would have just stayed where I was. But I might have floated away to who knows where. When I reentered my body, I crawled back into the torus and came back to Earth. I was there in Noland for … I don't know … less than a minute, same as the time before.

"When I go there again, …"

"When you go there again!" Grandma interrupted. "When?"

"In a few minutes. But don't worry, Grandma, I'll stay put. When I'm there, I'll be holding onto the end of the torus section so I won't drift away and get lost. But this time I'll be keeping in touch with it with only two fingers so that even more of my spirit-like self will be floating there in Noland."

Grandpa expounded, "Yes. We're now going to find out more about Molly's mysterious trips to Noland and then to Earth from Noland.

"But, let's make sure we all understand this. Evidently, first you go from Earth to Noland through the torus section. Then, even though you're holding onto it and hanging out into Noland, some kind of mysterious or spiritual part of you travels to another special place on Earth, the last place you were thinking about while in the torus. Right?"

Molly nodded in agreement. "Seems so."

"Okay, Molly, this time when you get to Earth from Noland, stay there for what you think is five minutes."

Grandma, who was gaining interest in these ventures and who now recognized the possible extraordinary importance of the torus section, made a suggestion for safety. "Let's tie some long cord around her ankle so that we can keep her connected with Earth in case she does break away and drifts out there."

"You really think that'll work?" Chel asked.

"And what about a cell phone?" Exi added. "It's worth a try, right?"

Grandpa said, "We can try it, but I don't think those things will work. I'll get some cord from the pantry. Any other ideas about keeping connected?"

Grandpa stood and took a step toward the pantry, then turned around. "Oh! Molly, what place will you be thinking about as you're crawling into Noland? A place we can easily get to from here."

"The kitchen."

◊

When Molly crawled through to reach into Noland, she had to yell, "I can't get there! It's blocked!"

"Here's why," Grandpa said, holding out the manual containing the ancient translations. "You can't use cords or anything else to go to Noland if they're long enough to stick out of both openings of the torus section. No such links can exist between our world and Noland. I bet phones won't work either."

Finally Molly crawled through without the cord and phone and disappeared into Noland, except for two fingers, which she used to hold onto the torus section.

They had agreed that when Molly entered Noland, they would head for the kitchen.

◊

"Oh my God, she looks like an angel! Oh my God!" Grandma cried out.

The four saw her floating near the ceiling, above the backyard door. They stood around in states of wonderment. Molly was not only weightless, she was semitransparent. She was wearing a long, white, flowing gown with full, flowing, white sleeves—nothing like what she was wearing when she entered the torus section for Noland. Then she drifted through the ceiling and floated into the backyard where she swirled among the flowers and trees, captivating her onlookers.

They watched her flow through the kitchen window back into the house and hover in front of the colorful curtains. Here the colors faintly showed through her, slightly obscuring her appearance. But this presentation was striking, emphasizing a celestial air about her. Molly gently floated around the kitchen, smiling at her family. Finally she winked at them and vanished through a kitchen wall toward the Rainbow Room.

All arrived in time to see her, in her usual human appearance, climb out of the torus section from where she had entered it. Sparkles jumped up to greet her.

◊

Once everyone was comfortably settled down, Chel shared her main observation. "You sure were a real ghost-like person, much more visible and lively than I saw before. Do you get better each time? I mean do you have more control?"

"Yes, I have better control each time. And I have less contact with the torus each time. Should I just let go? At least I'm going to practice to try to improve control of my spirit-like self when my spirit-like self goes to these special locations on Earth. This may have huge consequences for certain projects on Earth.

"Again, voices begged me to let go. But where would I go? I worry about what may happen if I just let go and find myself a hundred percent in Noland."

"Molly," Grandpa said, looking at his watch. "Those are great thoughts. But I think we've had enough for one day."

Molly was fascinated by all this. During the weekend, she went to Noland several times with the backing of Exi and Chel. She had been feeling an unusual significance as a blessed being in the torus section, and now she was beginning to understand that to function optimally, she must be free from any contact with it.

◊

That Sunday night, as Molly prepared for a sound sleep, she enjoyed thoughts about her new ability that could lead to humanitarian services on Earth. While she reclined comfortably, her imagination was in an exploratory mode.

What would happen if I did let go ... if I were completely detached from contact with the torus, which connects me with Earth? Where would I be? Who's there?

Her mind flashed to the Ladahalans from India, who disappeared centuries ago.

These people were the only ones who left any descriptions about the torus and where it leads. What did they know, and how did they know it?

It was certainly possible that the Ladahalans chose the name Noland to comply with whatever best described their experiences. There is no tangible evidence of such a place. No one can go into a place with no dimensions! Can they? There can't be such thing, can there? It's a non-place. But I was there! A magical "place" of some kind.

She finally fell asleep and had a dream.

She was standing on an infinitely large white floor that was her world. It had one boundary, an infinitely large white wall offering one closed door directly in front of her. She reached for the handle, pulled the door open, and took one step forward to be on the edge of this world for a maximum view of what reaches beyond.

She openly stretched an arm out into a clear sky. An irregularly shaped life-form floated toward her, tenderly waving. After a moment's hesitation, she waved back.

"Come on in," the engagingly musical voice from the figure said.

Molly pointed downward. "I can't! I'll fall!"

"You won't fall. You won't need wings. In fact, you won't need arms or legs … or even your whole body."

Molly saw an elusive, bright, pulsating form. It had no identifiable face nor any other familiar sign of life. It said, "We are the life forces of Noland. Because you are dreaming, we are in your head. Call us your dream spirits if you like."

Other dream spirits were drifting her way, beckoning her to enter.

"When you visit us, I will tell you some important things about Noland that will be to your benefit. I'll tell you one now. You will find out what an Earth angel really is!"

She dreamed she stepped through the door but held onto the wall from the outside with one hand. She was comfortably suspended in place. However, she could not see any part of her body. She felt almost nonexistent.

"Let go," the dream spirit said.

"I see, okay. Let me explain a few things. When you let go, you will still be in a spirit-like contact with us. All travel here in Noland is accomplished by concentration. You can go anywhere easily—anywhere in the world, and anywhere in Noland.

"And Molly, the reason you are dreaming is so that we can communicate more fully. When you wake up, please consider our conversations here in your dream and visit us. Now please let go."

Molly looked all around and saw hundreds of other dream spirits reaching for her.

"Molly, if you let go of the wall and completely come in, you will find that you'll be able to help solve serious problems on Earth. You only need to think about a place that needs your worthy help and you'll be there.

"Please come in. There is so much that a blessed soul can do for his or her world from here." A lengthy silence followed the dream spirit's plea.

Molly noticed the dream spirit smiling and slowly backing away, and she saw the others smiling with hope and gesturing with both arms and hands for her to enter as they backed off too.

Finally, as her dream was coming to a close, she let go of the wall.

When Molly awoke in the morning, she scrambled to see Exi and Chel. "There's gotta be something truly amazing about Noland. I'm going to let go!"

◊

Chel overheard an odd conversation at school later that Monday. She met with her sister after school to explain.

"Exi, this was a little spooky. I was in a classroom, near the door, and looking for a book I'd left behind, when I heard a boy and girl talking in the hallway by the lockers. The boy asked, 'Do you know where the dogfights are going to be tomorrow night? I'd like to go.' She told him that she heard her father talking about it. She said that it would be at the abandoned something building. Sounded like she said the *Creyox* building."

This aroused Exi. "Wow, the cops have been trying for months to put a stop to that stuff. You overheard some important information."

Chel continued, "So I asked around and found out that there is an old, abandoned building on the east side of town called the Grey Box Building. That should be it. Should we call the cops?"

"Yeah. But I don't want us getting so involved that we'd have to face these villains in court. Hmm ... we need to think this through. But for now let's keep low."

◇

That Tuesday night, the old Grey Box Building was quiet and dark. The windows were firmly boarded shut, and there were no interior lights visible from the outside. But people were sneaking in through an opened back door. They were entering a large room with a high ceiling and scores of chairs circling a large dog pit.

Exi and Chel hid in a dark corner down the block to watch them enter. Finally, the door closed.

The dog pit room was smoky and smelled like stale tobacco, pot, beer, and dog feces. The sounds were ferocious. A bull terrier and a mastiff were in the ring ripping into each other, and their piercing growls and cries were mixing with the watchers' yells. "Kill 'im Ripper!" "No—I got fifty on Racer!" "Git 'im Racer!" "Kill 'im, kill 'im! …" The fight was vicious. Each dog was fighting for his life, as trained.

Suddenly the dogs stopped fighting and faced upward toward the high ceiling. This puzzled the spectators. They looked up to see what the dogs were staring at. The sudden termination of a serious dog fight is supposed to result from a downed or dead dog, so this was a bizarre happening. At first they didn't see anything unusual, but evidently the dogs did.

Then they experienced a flash of intense brightness near the ceiling. It was the dawn of a beautiful angel who began hovering high above the crowd of cruelty. She was stretched out and smiling downward. She was huge—about thirty feet long and proportionately wide. Her large white gown with wide outstretched sleeves was flowing.

This was just the introduction. She first focused on the fight in the pit, then on the crowd. Her smile soured.

Her frown increased until her mouth flew open with a yelp of great fear. Her eyes transformed into the wide eyes of a frightened dog. Her wings became huge dog paws with extended claws, aggressively thrashing toward the crowd as if in a fearful defensive state of trying to reverse her slow descent toward the crowd. She was growling fearfully, and her opened snout sprouted vampire-like fangs that extended outward to meet the onlookers and protect herself from their cruelty.

The heartless onlookers panicked at the sight of such approaching viciousness. Chaos followed. Each was shoving another to scramble out of the building. People were running over fallen people, and some of the fallen struggled to their feet only to push another down.

But they were not as strong as the force of police they encountered as they streamed out onto the parking lot. In fact, many welcomed the police at this stage.

Then something interrupted the encounter. Sheer beauty flowed through the walls into the air above the crowd. Her smile spoke of forgiveness. Her wings spread massively, extending over the entire parking lot, and she reached down and extended waves to all.

The mouths of the dog watchers opened in awe as they gazed upward. Then all in the parking lot became still and silent until many gave a shy wave in return.

Then she vanished.

◊

The three met in the Rainbow Room to discuss the evening's events, and, as typical of their get-togethers, Sparkles joined them.

"That was great, Molly," Chel said. "They finally got what they deserved."

Exi chimed in. "Yeah, we timed it just right. Chel and I called 911 the second you waved your wing through the wall. But Molly, tell us what you experienced. What did you see?"

"I mainly saw the fighting, and I felt the fear of the dogs. That made my task easier." She looked at Sparkles, who was sniffing the torus section, and she softened her words. "I love dogs." She focused on the torus section and said no more, and in a few seconds, she smiled.

"Yeah," Chel said, also glancing at Sparkles. "Hopefully, those creeps won't ever go back to dog fighting." Eyeing Molly, she said, "What are you pondering now, Molly?"

Molly, now in thought about the mystifying nature of her trip, replied, "Noland. When I was finished and in the air above the parking lot, I knew it was time to return.

"I saw the dream spirit. She ... or he, or whatever ... was waving and welcoming me back to Noland. Then hundreds of these beings approached me from all around and waved. I felt a loving warmth— kinda like hugs. It seemed like I was floating in a dream, and as I came near the torus, I turned and waved back. I looked all around and wondered about what kind of existence this could really be. Maybe I was becoming a bit more sensitive that such a strange realm of existence really does exist. Impulsively, I said, 'I would like to come back to Noland sometime, just for a visit.' I'll never forget her reply: 'You will always be welcome here in your new land, Molly.' And they all added a little extra gusto to their waves as I returned home to Earth."

The House at
the Beach

The journeys through the torus confirmed Grandma and Grandpa's earlier suspicions about Molly's otherworldly connections. The few months of growing affection for Molly and the realization that she really didn't have a home as we know it led them to make some sensitive inquiries. But nowhere in their research into areas of parapsychology, spiritualism, mind-over-matter, life elsewhere in the universe, and so on, did they ever find a hint of such a real unworldly experience, at least not so close to the their own here and now. Following their hearts' desires, and their granddaughters' convincing guidance, they happily and informally adopted her as a granddaughter, and provided her with a comfortable upstairs bedroom overlooking their neatly cared-for backyard.

Molly still maintained her house on the green lawn in the forest near the yellow rose. She regularly returned to continue her explorations of the universe through the enhanced telescope. Often Exi and Chel would join her. They were becoming increasingly fascinated with what they were noticing in the great beyond, witnessing wonders they had never before imagined. Molly loved probing the cosmos. She longed for occasions when she could be out there.

This evening Exi and Chel were at their grandparents' home and planned to spend the night in the spare bedroom. They spent most of the evening with Molly discussing the beauty and wonders of the cosmos before going to bed. They had planned to visit the telescope first thing in the morning, but that didn't happen.

◊

Everyone was waking up and preparing to trek down to the kitchen, where each was to contribute in the preparation of breakfast under Grandma's guidance. Exi was the first to arrive downstairs. She was about to open the front door to check the weather when she noticed Sparkles standing on the seat of a chair that was backed up to the dining room front window. His front paws were propped up on the chair's back, but he needed to look around the side of the chair for an outside view. He was focused on something, and his tail was not wagging. "What are you looking at, boy?" Exi asked as she opened the door.

Everyone heard Exi's terrifying scream and came rushing downstairs to see what the matter was. All huddled at the front door and gazed out upon a seemingly impossible transformation. Their neat, grassy front yard was gone. Instead, they were staring at an ocean and its wide beach.

The beach rose toward them from the ocean's edge up to a twenty-foot wide grassy mound. A few feet in from the mound sat the front of the house. The sun hovered peacefully over the horizon. All this would have presented a gorgeous view and an ideal location for a house if not for the present circumstances. The five standing at the door were horrified.

Grandpa said, "What in the Lord's name is happening? Stand back! I'm closing the door." Emotions of dread filled the air.

Each side of the house offered a view of the grassy mound, and from the kitchen window, the backyard seemed smooth and well-kept. Surrounding the backyard was an impressive work of beauty—a deep pine forest.

The five gathered at the kitchen table. Exi and Chel were crying. "We've got to figure this out," Grandma announced. "I noticed something else. There is no car and no driveway, not even a road."

"And no neighbors," Exi added.

"We have telephones," Grandpa said. "I'm calling 911." He picked up the kitchen phone and dialed. "The phone's dead." The others scrambled for their cells, but none worked.

"We've become isolated," Chel mumbled, expressing her dread of entrapment.

Grandpa tried to sound normal. "We need to think and explore this and come up with a plan to save ourselves. Oh, Lord, what are we into?"

They began their planning over a simple breakfast to give them the energy to explore. Their first target was the grassy mound, and they agreed to stay together.

They considered items they would need for such a mission. Grandpa retrieved his compass from the tool drawer in the kitchen, but when he opened it, he saw that the dial was continuously spinning counterclockwise. He asked everyone to check their watches and other timepieces. One old wind-up clock worked. Exi dashed to her computer and found that she could not go online, but her offline functionality was fine.

Molly offered the striking observation, "It seems like the objects that don't work depend on things that are far away."

Grandpa asked Grandma to see if the oven worked while he checked the TV and a radio. The oven did work, but the TV and radio did not. Grandpa said, "You're right, Molly. You're onto something, but I don't know what yet."

Molly said, "There are no telephone poles or power lines outside like in our normal neighborhood. But we do have electricity. Oh, and we have running water," adding to the mystery. Summing up the situation, she said, "Oh, we are in some kinda trouble!"

All were silent for a moment, pondering over what all this meant. Gradually, Exi, Chel, and their grandparents turned to face Molly.

Molly briefly hesitated before presenting her daring perspective: "All that we're experiencing suggests that we are not on Earth."

The other four just stared at her with wide eyes and open mouths.

"Moreover, I'd say that something is supplying us with electricity and water, because that something wants us to have these necessities. But it's not supplying us with land lines for the house phones, TV, and other things that are not necessary for life."

Grandma needed clarification. "Molly, you're so technical that it's hard for me to follow. And, of course, it's hard for me to believe we are not on Earth. How can that be?"

Molly covered her mouth with her hands. "I know. I'm sorry, Grandma. I don't have a better explanation."

"I have a thought," Grandma exclaimed. If we're at some faraway place, then maybe Molly can ... But wait ... what did we do with the torus?"

"Ah, the torus," Grandpa said. "Great thought, Lyn. But no, it's at the shop."

$$\Diamond$$

Grandpa announced, "The morning's moving on. We need to conduct our exploration." They checked their house keys and found that they worked. They locked the door behind them and took a few steps out onto the grassy mound.

"Should we go north or south?" Grandpa asked.

Molly responded. "Which direction is north?"

Grandpa faced the ocean and pointed to the left.

"That's assuming we're facing east and that the sun here rises in the east." Molly said. "If we're not on Earth, the sun may rise differently. And anyway, what's east? Moreover, what's the sun?" Being from the planet Friend, Molly was greatly aware of planet differences and wanted everyone to be open to subtle changes from earthly familiarities.

They turned left. The plan was to walk for about half an hour, paying careful attention to their surroundings. Grandpa took the lead, with Sparkles on his leash. Because Sparkles had been the first to notice the change in their surroundings, they planned to monitor his reactions as they moved along. They would return in the same manner and further explore the other direction. Later they would explore the edge of the pine forest bordering the backyard. There was much to explore.

Sparkles, with perked ears, occasionally would stop and face the pine forest bordering the grassy mound. Each time Grandma would ask, "Does anyone hear anything?" No one did. This pattern continued on the return trip as well until, at about halfway home, Sparkles suddenly barked and tried to dash to the forest. Fortunately, Grandpa had a sturdy grasp on his leash.

They quietly gazed into the forest for a minute but saw nothing unusual. They agreed not to creep in and continued on their way.

As they neared the house, Molly commented that nothing spectacular had occurred, with the exception of Sparkles's reactions to something in the forest. Just then something caught Chel's eye. "What's that?" she asked, pointing to the horizon over the ocean.

They stopped and faced the ocean. The crest of a massive yellow sphere was beginning to rise over the horizon. As it rose, its size became more impressive. They watched this breathtaking event for twenty minutes until all of it was above the horizon.

"It can't be another sun," Molly said. "It's not that bright. It must be some kind of supermoon, but … it's the size of ten suns, not accounting for distance." She kept staring. "Impressive, wow!"

"And it's moving pretty fast," Grandma said. "You're right, Molly, we're not on Earth!"

◊

After a late lunch and short rest, the team, including Sparkles, went through the backyard to the forest's edge. Up close they were in a better position to note its beauty, despite their fears of the unknowns dimming their views.

None of them recognized this species of pine tree. The pines were spaced twenty to thirty feet apart and were unusually tall. The forest was bright. The clear sky was easily seen between the treetops. Grandpa took one step in. The ground was flat, soft, and covered with sweet-smelling pine needles. All was still except for the enormous moon, which was floating closer toward them as they faced the forest.

They walked around the backyard and studied the forest as far as they could peer into it. Sparkles seemed eager to journey in. At one point he stopped and faced the forest, but this time he wagged his tail.

"He senses something friendly in there," Exi said. "Maybe we could walk in a little. We can follow Sparkles and see what he's wagging at."

Grandpa replied, "Okay, as long as we keep the house in view. We don't have a compass, and if we get lost, we're in big trouble."

They cautiously ventured into the forest under Sparkles's lead. Each one occasionally turned to make sure the house was in view. The pines were spaced sparsely enough that the family could proceed inward many yards and keep their bearings. Finally, Sparkles stopped and focused on something straight ahead. At first, no one could see anything out of the ordinary. Then Exi pointed. "There. Something short among the tall trees. A baby pine?"

"No," Molly said, "it's not the right shape."

"It's not moving," Grandpa said. "Seems safe. If Sparkles is willing, we'll move in a little closer and see what it is. Okay, Lyn?"

"Yes. We came in here to explore—to see what we can understand about our predicament."

Sparkles walked alongside the others. Within a few yards of the object, Exi recognized it. "Stop!" she screamed. "It's a monkey!"

The monkey faced their way and was motionless. It was standing in a posture resembling a long distance runner leaning forward and waiting for the shot that starts the race. All gazed in astonishment, and it never flinched. "It's a statue," Grandma said.

"I don't know," Molly replied. "It looks real. But maybe you're right. Any living animal moves at least slightly, even while sleeping. And this is crouching."

"Let's move a little closer," Grandpa said, "but very slowly."

They formed a tight line and inched in. Finally they were within six feet of it. It was staring, with bright red eyes, straight ahead at Grandma, who was at the center of the line.

Exi was standing on the right end with a tight hold on Sparkles's leash when she screamed. "Oh my God, its eyes shifted! It's staring at Sparkles! It's alive!"

Just then the light among the pines dimmed, and in a few seconds it became apparent that darkness was quickly creeping in.

"What's happening now?" Grandpa asked. "Are we getting trapped? Maybe we should go back to the house."

"No!" Grandma said forcefully. "We must stand our ground, or else we'll be lost."

They found themselves near a strange object in a strange forest, surrounded by darkness. Sparkles howled, and then he whimpered. The others were just as frightened.

"Oh help us, please," Grandpa prayed. "Is this the way night comes here?"

Everyone sat down, and they all tightly held hands, occasionally giving one another a squeeze. Several minutes transpired before Molly unraveled the mystery. "Oh, it's a total eclipse of the sun! That giant moon came between us and the sun ... I think."

Then a bit of light peeked through the trees. "Thank God," Grandma said.

When it became lighter, the motionless monkey was positioned as before, but his gaze was shifting from person to person. But the family was shocked to find that something new had been added to the environment. They were encircled by a large crowd of monkeys—moving monkeys, maybe fifty of them. The nearest was strolling toward them.

$$\Diamond$$

"Stay calm," its voice said. "We are kind beings. We are the higher life forms on this planet.

"I see you all are frightened, but really, I must prove to you that you can trust us. My name is Carl. You all have been sent here to help us. Especially Molly. And all of you will be duly rewarded."

"Here to help? You know us? I ... I don't understand." Grandpa shook as he stuttered. "And ... Molly?"

Carl said to the other monkeys, "Okay, you may go now." They turned and scattered away in all directions.

The earthlings saw that the monkeys, including the motionless monkey, were wearing dark brown shirts and pants.

To the family, Carl said, "I had to make sure you didn't panic and bolt. That's why the others were here—to make sure you stayed here until we could meet."

Molly thoughtfully changed the course of conversation. "You … speak … English."

"Oh, yes. Thanks for reminding me. We had to learn English and much more about your culture in order to be able to communicate with you. How did we learn all this? you may ask. We are quick and thorough learners, and we are extraordinarily intelligent." He paused. "And another thing: we aren't monkeys."

"We can see that now," Grandpa said.

"In fact, we've become extraordinarily gifted over the millions of years that we've existed, despite our appearance to you. We were the first intelligent life ever created after the big bang. We may not appear to be as technically advanced as earthlings or friendlings. But we amronians don't need to be …"

Molly's mouth fell open as she interrupted. "You know about the friendlings?"

The five earthlings now had many questions. Their fears were diminishing as curiosities were emerging.

"Yes, we know the friendlings," Carl replied. "But we have a different kind of advancement from them. You need to learn more about us, and then I'll explain your visit here.

"We rely largely on our parapsychological and spiritual capabilities. Therefore we are able, to a limited extent, to communicate with higher beings. It's mental communication, which happens rarely. Anyway, between our powerful psychic techniques and our rare communications with the higher beings, we amronians can do remarkable things that match and sometimes exceed what the friendlings can do with their advanced science and technology.

"You may think of our techniques as being similar to what you may envision as real magic." His eyes met Grandpa's eyes. "But we do some science too, which of course helps."

Carl extended his hand, and the others warily responded. Sparkles, after some backing off, finally allowed Carl to pet him.

◊

An interesting and important question occurred to Grandma. "Carl, from early this morning until now, for seven or eight hours, we lived in confusion and fear. Why didn't you meet us up front—early? That would have prevented ..."

"We couldn't do that," Carl interrupted. "Six of us had to observe you all for a while. We had to see how each of you would respond to petrifying situations, to being suddenly exposed to unbelievable unknowns, such as a new world. Each of us has special gifts. Two of us are superior perception analysts. We have ways of seeing and listening in order to sense things about each of you. For a while we were spies. But now we are trusting teammates. Soon you will see why all this was necessary.

"Once you almost caught us. That was when you were heading home from your exploration near the beach this morning and we were hiding nearby. Sparkles somehow sensed us and barked, and we just froze."

"Yeah," Grandpa said, wondering what would have happened had they had followed Sparkles's lead.

Carl continued. "The six of us had a meeting and decided each of you passed the 'fear' test, which we were pretty sure you would do. That means each of you is up to the task, especially Molly, who will be directly involved in the mission."

Molly took a step back. "What task? What mission? What are you talking about?"

Carl hesitated before speaking. "First I must give you some background. I know you all: Chel, Exi, Molly, Lyn, and Roger. I know you are frightened and confused. Yes, and you too, sweet Sparkles. But I want to assure you that you are safe, and in fact, you are protected. For a short time you will be on this planet, Amron, which is very far from Earth. Amron is not in your solar system with your other planets. In fact it's not even in the Milky Way. It's in another galaxy, many millions of light years away from Earth. And Amron is about the size of Earth.

"And we are on a large island of Amron: Pine Island. Yes, your house is on Pine Island, millions of light years from its location on Earth. The place where your house and yard were located on Earth is replaced by a three-dimensional solid image of your house and property—a solid hologram if you will. This ensures that passersby will not become alarmed by a sudden vacant lot. Besides, we have our eyes on it.

"But you and your lovely home will safely return the day after tomorrow. Then you will receive your reward. You might feel as though you've been kidnapped, but that will change. You are here to bring about a great humanitarian feat on Amron and to save many lives. Soon you will understand."

The humans' eyes widened. "Humanitarian feat?" Chel cried out.

"What … what do you mean?" Grandma asked. "What can a small family from Earth do so far away, on another planet?"

Carl did not answer.

Although the conversation was fascinating, all were curious as to what their mission was on Amron, and why they had been chosen for it. This curiosity spilled out from Exi. "Why are we here? What's Molly supposed to do?"

"I will explain that to you. But first, let's get out of the forest before it starts to become dark. Let's go to your house where we'll be comfortable and have some dinner. Then we will discuss your mission. A nice roast beef with potatoes and carrots awaits us in the oven."

"Somehow that does not surprise me," Chel mumbled, with wide-open eyes and raised eyebrows.

$$\Diamond$$

"Okay, here we go," Carl said upon getting comfortable with the others in the dining room to discuss the mission while consuming a scrumptious five-star dinner.

"We amronians on Pine Island have a big problem. The first amronian you saw, the motionless one, well, we had to temporarily paralyze him. Spavor is his name. Spavor was becoming evil. He was beginning to do horrible things. He would steal things from other amronians. He would try to fight us, and he tried to steal the wives of some male amronians, and break up families.

We are by and large a crimeless society. Oh, some small crimes occasionally occur, but nothing major. But as for Spavor, we just had to contain him. This has happened to a lesser extent to other amronians over the last five years, but they recovered with some help.

"Five years ago an evil presence landed here. Maybe 'landed' isn't the best word. I can describe it better later, but our explorers have learned that this evil presence slithered out of a small hole from under a rock, assumed colors of its surroundings, and snaked around until it learned some things about us. Then it just appeared one day, first as a seemingly nice young boy who walked around with a smile and a limp. In the beginning, he would introduce himself by saying things like, 'Hi, I'm Mr. Evil.' At first we thought he was just a wacky little kid. But he—or it—proved to be pure evil. We found that this Mr. Evil assumes different forms, such as elderly women, philosophers, and pets, for example, depending on its plan or pleasure.

"We've experienced evil here before, but not one that was a breathing being, and so in-your-face. We found that he was trying to make Spavor insane—trying to make him want to commit murder. We are a challenge for this Mr. Evil, and he likes challenges. He wants to battle us, to make us all evil. He comes into some of our homes at night and waves his arms before us and utters unintelligible chants. That's one of the ways he tries to make us evil.

"Yet we are not able to destroy him.

"And with children …! He comes along as a 'nice wise man' and convinces children that they would have a better life if only they were dishonest and lied about things when it's to their advantage. For example, suppose a kid wants more money. This nice wise man might tell them things like: 'Your parents don't give you enough. How unfair. You're just going to have to do this on your own. Look, there's a bowl of tip money down at the take-out, right down there. Go there and take some. Take it all; you deserve it. That's life, man. Grow up!' Yeah, this Mr. Evil does things like that and worse things to our children … to all of us.

"We have temporarily made Spavor deaf so that Mr. Evil's chants are ineffective. But we're counseling him, so during these sessions we return his hearing. When Mr. Evil has been destroyed, Spavor should be fine again. We must fight back, and we will.

"And we will win. Molly will do that for us!"

"Whoa!" cried Molly. "Do what? ... Oh, I can't battle ..."

"No, no," interrupted Carl. "You aren't going to fight him physically. Just getting near him should do it. He'll try to get away from you. We believe that if you just touch him, that would destroy him."

"But why me? Why don't your higher beings take care of this?"

"The higher beings have implied that it is the duty of planetary beings to fight evil among themselves. They never explained why, but some amronian scholars say that if evil didn't exist for us, then we wouldn't know evil, and that would weaken an important essence of our being. They argue that if evil didn't exist among planetary beings, then there could not be an understanding of goodness. Where would that leave us? That means evil exists, and in this case it's right on top of us, and we need to fight it.

"'And why me?' you ask," Carl continued, looking at Molly. "There are a few reasons. First, because of your character. We all know of the superior character possessed by friendlings. The power of their character is manifested in all physical parts of their bodies. Friendlings possess the strongest and most beautiful personalities and souls of any beings in the universe.

"Especially you, Molly. In your childhood, you were transferred alone to a foreign planet—Earth. And as you were struggling to make a home of it, your character grew. It grew a lot. Not to the level of a higher being, of course, but ... well ... we don't quite know what you are. Oh! I mean ... Sorry. You are a nice human girl too.

"Anyway, you grew into some kind of a superior integrity, a powerful threat to evil.

"Yes, Molly, you are a threat to evil. Mr. Evil will acquire a sense of dread and weakness if ... when ... he sees you up close."

"Oh my ... Oh my!" Molly was shaking. Grandma was holding one of her hands, and Carl took the other.

"And the reason for your family coming along is to support you. All of them have experienced unusual, otherworldly adventures with you. Together you comprise the ideal team."

Molly remained silent.

"You will be fine, Molly. He cannot hurt you; he cannot get near you. Just the smell of your blood would kill him. But beware: He's always aggressive. Although he's mean and the essence of evil, we're sure you will win."

"So what's the plan?" Exi asked distrustfully.

Carl's positive expression faded. "We've had trouble tracking him. We can't catch him. He doesn't live in any one hole. But when Spavor was confined and guarded to keep him safe, Mr. Evil found a spot nearby and somehow made a hole deep in the ground. We can't block it. He blows away any covering. And it appears to be infinitely deep." Carl nodded to Molly. "Let me explain something about these holes that should be useful to earthlings, and to beings elsewhere for that matter, so you all will understand the big picture. Then you'll be ready."

$$\Diamond$$

"Mr. Evil travels. He's often here and there at the same time. He splits himself into various parts, and each part can go on a mission in a different world. He changes, expands, takes on hidden appearances, and operates secretly sometimes and boldly other times. How does he get to these different worlds? Our explorers say he travels through underground holes, then through ... well, I should be careful here ... realms of hollow gravity!

"All things—all mass—exhibits gravity, which permeates the galaxies of the universe. The farther apart two heavenly bodies are, the less the shared gravitational effects. They have very little pull on each other. On the other hand, a black hole is a mass that is so dense that it gravitates even light into it. That's why we can't see it. Light coming near it gets sucked right into it. Powerful gravity there, huh? So gravity is everywhere, weak in some places and strong in others.

"Will you explain this more, please? Just joking!" Carl said to Chel.

"Take your planet, for example. Mr. Evil travels down one of his holes to the center of Earth. From there, he takes a path to the center of another occupied planet elsewhere in the universe. Earthlings know very little about the Earth's interior. In fact they know much more about outer space than about Earth's own inner space. If you picture the Earth as an apple, then explorers have not yet probed below its peel and argue that any future approach to the core is impossible. The very centers of all planets have a 'hollow gravity.' It's the location where gravity from the rest of the planet pulls equally. The masses of a planet's sun, moons, and other bodies in space have a role in this too, but that effect is miniscule at the planet's center, which is surrounded by the planet's own mass. But the relatively small gravitational effects of those other bodies, the planet's rotation, and other factors cause minor changes in the size and location of the planet's most central realm: the place of the hollow gravity.

"This is where the higher geometries of space-time come in. Mr. Evil resides in and loves hollow gravity. The places of hollow gravity throughout the universe are connected by a maze of channels or pathways comprised of the interaction of gravity and the accelerated universal expansion in the cosmos. This way, Mr. Evil reaches the centers and therefore the populations of the inhabited worlds. Mr. Evil travels through these channels with speeds that equal simultaneity. That kinda gives you the gist of it.

"Next let me explain something you all should know. Remember the hole I mentioned earlier near Spavor. That's a way to hollow gravity, to Amron's center and beyond. He takes naps somewhere in there in the early afternoons. We know he'll be in his hole then. So tomorrow I'll come here to your house and bring lunch, and after lunch I'll lead you to his hole. We don't know what he will look like then. He surely will try to scare you, but that's when the battle begins."

"Oh sure!" Chel cried. "Molly attacks some unknown …"

"Chel," Carl interrupted, "remember we discussed that. Molly will be safe, and she will win."

He asked Molly, "Will you help us? I beg you … please?"

"Yes."

Carl added, "We here will always love you.

"So before lunch tomorrow, trim your finger- and toenails and cut some of your hair. Your body parts contain the essence of your blessed character, so they will be good weapons against evil. If some of that touches this evil, whatever appearance it has when you see it should destroy him. If he sees you are there to fight him, I wouldn't be surprised if he takes on some familiar Earthlike form to catch you off guard, such as a young, enchanting teenage boy with a fetish for you. But you have to remember: Whatever he looks like, you have to destroy him. Will you do that, Molly?"

"My nails? Hair?"

"Molly, your whole you—your essence—has been blessed by almighty powers. Evidence has been seen. Your hair and nails are part of all of you. Some of these are easily removed, so that blessedness can touch and be felt by Mr. Evil."

Molly hesitated. "Okay."

"So will you do that?"

"Yes," Molly said unsteadily. "I'll do it."

"Thank you dearly, Molly."

Carl stood up. "Okay, folks, I'll see you here tomorrow."

Grandma said appreciatively, "Thank you for creating dinner, Carl. It was delicious."

When Carl left, Grandma said to Molly, "You can back out at any time, you know. You understand that, don't you?"

"I know," Molly replied. "But I do believe Carl. This is such a major mission, and so much planning has gone into it. It seems that only I can do this worthwhile deed. I'm up to it. I just wonder how I'm supposed to get near this Mr. Evil. Guess I'll find out tomorrow."

◊

"Mr. Evil's hole is in the forest, about a hundred yards past Spavor," Carl said as they finished lunch. "Molly, do you have your trimmings? I see you look different, though still very pretty."

Molly held up a transparent storage bag. "Here they are. Last night Grandma gave me a major haircut so that I would have plenty of hair for the mission."

Carl led the way out through the back door and into the forest. They slowly passed Spavor, whose eyes focused on Molly. Two other amronians were consoling him, and they nodded as Molly and crew passed by.

"Spavor knows," Carl announced. "When some of us are with him, we allow him to hear. We keep him posted on what's happening. He feels less abandoned that way. Between that and the reassurances, he's fine now, but we need to keep him away from Mr. Evil's influence. He's still vulnerable."

They kept marching deeper into the forest with little conversation. The smell of sulfur began to permeate the air. Finally Carl slowed down and pointed ahead. "A few more yards. You see it? Some messy dirt and the hole."

The group slowly pressed on with Molly taking the lead, clutching her bag to her chest. But they were brought to a sudden halt by booming shouts of madness.

"Who's out there?! *Out, out, outa* here!"

Everyone froze. They first saw two long, thick horns emerging from the hole. Then they saw the head. It was the size and shape of a forty-pound bag of compact manure. Mr. Evil's face was a deep red, and his bright red eyes flared like fire. His nose puffed with angry breaths, and his scowling mouth drooped, exposing two long, glittery fangs.

He crawled out growling and stood in front of his hole. He faced the crowd, his long arrow-tipped tail thrusting from side to side, sweat oozing from his naked ten-foot tall body. He scanned the group while sniffing. Then he focused on Molly, aiming his fifteen-foot long pitchfork at her. Fire shot from his mouth with his nasty speech.

"You leave now, you stinking little bitch, or you're going to be hanging from these prongs! Out! Now!"

Molly screamed at him: "I'll dodge it, spit on it, and pitch it down your hole. The higher spirits have damned you as pure evil, and I'm proud to have a part in your destruction!"

The others were amazed at this show of courage, and so was the evil persona.

Just as Mr. Evil began drawing back his pitchfork to hurl it, Molly charged, and, within six feet of him, she spit at him. He immediately jumped backward and dropped into his hole as the spit fell short. Molly ran up to the hole.

Carl urgently countered, "Molly, careful! The hole!"

Molly yelled, "Pieces of me will meet you down there, devil."

Just as she was about to toss some fingernail and hair trimmings down the hole, she heard the fearful cry of a little girl and saw the girl's bleeding hands struggling to climb out of the hole. "Oh, God ... help! Oh please help me!" Molly was stunned and immediately backed off, as the girl's panic was further expressed by her face, now bobbing around at ground level. Eyes say it all. The pleading for life was there, and Molly immediately recognized her younger sister, Hollyholtright from Friend, whom she loved and missed so much.

Holly was one of the few friendlings who never wanted Molly to leave. She loved everyone, and was recognized as an especially high-spirited being of love and hope. Even at such a young age, Holly was one of the many friendlings who opened to life's mission of fighting evil. And she was especially adamant about it. One of the reasons that there was less evil on Friend than on most worlds was on account of beings like her. But only Molly embodied the miraculous ability to face real supernatural encounters—an ability she had recently recognized. While her sister Holly did not have such otherworldly spiritual potential, she had the moxie, an attribute Molly had always admired. Yet, understandably, Molly was mystified by how all this could be. How could she even get here?

As Molly took a step closer to Holly's reaching hand, Carl and the others began screaming about her nearness to the hole of hell. Carl began running to grab her. Suddenly, Molly flung her trimmings into Holly's upward-pleading face. Holly's face fractured and melted while spilling out its vile cries of hatred. Blurred shapes of horns poked out from where the eyes were, then shattered into invisible pieces. The arm and hand that was begging for help extended outward to grab Molly before shriveling up, and smoke towered from the hole as the withering body slithered downward.

The ground near the hole was beginning to tremble, and from deep down, grumbling afterthoughts echoed: "Aah ... uh ... I ... wanna ... kill ..." Being careful to not lean directly over the hole, Molly skillfully lobbed a mouthful of spit through it. Within seconds there was silence.

The silence continued while Carl, Grandpa, Grandma, Exi, and Chel were stretched on the ground, waiting for who knows what. Molly slowly backed off on her hands and knees. Suddenly a bright light flashed from the hole, followed quickly by a deafening boom. A ball of fire shot out toward the sky. It increased in size and kept rising at a tremendous speed. Many miles up it exploded with the force and blinding brightness of a nuclear bomb. After the explosion, as all was becoming still, billions of twinkles decorated the sky, as if accommodating celestial praise.

As all was settling, everyone's sight shifted toward the enormous rising moon.

Exi and Chel were each on one side of Molly, holding her hands while gazing into the sky. The huge moon peacefully sailed through. Each would swear that the following happened, although no one else witnessed anything like it:

The faint outline of a face on the passing moon looked at them. Its mouth opened, and as if whispering in each girl's right ear, the moon said, "Don't worry, I'll collect any ashes and get rid of them." The moon seemed to stop for a second. "But just remember: Evil's offshoots still dwell in the hollow places." An outline of an arm extended and waved. Then the moon rotated and faced the direction it was moving in and continued on.

As the brief eclipse of the sun followed, Exi expressed a sentiment that all three felt. "What kind of amazing world are we in?"

Carl, Grandma, and Grandpa stepped over to hold Molly and to express their feelings of admiration. Molly began to feel a homelike presence when she looked down and saw Sparkles begging for her arms and smiling.

Just then, an amronian with open arms came running up to Molly. "Oh Molly! I love you. I'm Spavor. You saved my life, my soul. I thank you oh so much!"

This was a beautiful moment for Molly. "I helped. It was really your people who saved you partially though me. And my family gave me their much-needed presence and support. But really, Spavor, thank your angels."

◊

Carl walked the family back to the house. They sat on beach chairs on the grassy mound, facing the ocean, enjoying the cool breeze, and reviewing the afternoon's feat. Carl's eyes backed his words. "Thank you all so much. Molly. You are so courageous, and you have prevented evil from spreading among us amronians. We all sincerely thank you."

"If another Mr. Evil comes, you know where to find me," Molly offered with an honest smile.

"Oh, one more thing, folks," Carl added. "Your reward is ready for you on Earth."

"And what is that?" Chel asked.

"It's something that all of you have wanted for a long time, especially beach-bum Molly: A house at the beach."

"Oh my God!" Chel screamed. "We have so wanted that." Molly began jumping up and down, and laughing and clapping with joy, while Exi was grinning from ear-to-ear and pumping her fists into the air. All in the family registered shock, but in a minute they calmed down enough to manage a sincere warm hug for Carl.

"It's at the beach you all go to. You'll love it. The keys and all the paperwork will be on the kitchen table at your home in the morning. Oh, and there's a special kind of phone there too. All you need to do is push the button to connect with faraway me. Have a good night's sleep, and when you wake up in the morning, things will be back to normal. You and your beautiful home will again be safely resting on Earth. And hey, enjoy your new beach house!"

This time when they woke up and Exi ran downstairs, Sparkles was looking out front through the dining room window, tail a-wagging. And Exi did not scream like a crazed witness to unworldly transformations when she opened the front door. This time when the family sat down for breakfast, no one felt panicked. In fact, a few minutes later, they felt overjoyed when Grandma stood up to remove the empty scrambled eggs platter and announced: "Pack up family. We're heading for the beach!"

What's out There?

Grandpa was frolicking around with Sparkles in the living room. As usual, Sparkles was loving it. Grandpa was too.

"Our beach trip was short, wasn't it boy? But the house was there, huh?" That was the main purpose of the trip: to see if it really existed. Grandpa and Grandma were planning another trip to their new beach house when schedules would allow for a longer stay and would include visits from family members and friends. Some talk focused on inviting Carl.

But now was a relaxing break. Grandpa had time to unwind and more time to ponder the miraculous changes occurring in their lives. It seemed as though Molly's transformation from another world to a member of their household opened the family auras of otherworldly perceptions. The only other time Grandpa had physically experienced anything nearly resembling signs of supernatural or spiritual life was when he was nine years old, but that was a brief encounter that did not resemble Molly's presence. So, in addition to his earlier inquiries, what else could he do to find out more about these things that "peek" into the world he knew? Who should he and Grandma confidently consult with about Molly and "other worlds?" How should he approach Molly about his questions, and when? Or should he? Anyway, he was now pleased to be home with some time for contemplation and relaxation.

"Hey boy!" he said to Sparkles, smiling and reaching for the rope toy.

"Go get it, boy!" Sparkles loved to chase his rope toy. Grandpa would grab the free end of it and fling it down the hallway or into another room, putting a decent upward arc on it so that the hard rubber ball on the other end would have a fun bounce when it hit the floor. Sparkles went for the bounce. He would bounce with it for a while. Then when this dance was over, he would grab the rope with his teeth and slap the ball from cheek to cheek while running back to Grandpa for another round. Sometimes Grandpa would tease him by spinning the rope toy at a high speed as if he were going to sling it mightily across the street. This is what he was doing when it accidentally left his hand and crashed noisily through the living room window.

"Don't worry, I'll fix it," Grandpa called out while staring through the broken pane, knowing that Grandma was nearing the entrance to the living room.

"The girls will be here shortly," Grandma announced before heading back to the Rainbow Room. "They want to play with Sparkles—responsibly, of course. Make sure that all the glass is safely discarded."

Much of the glass appeared to have sailed outside with the rope toy. Other pieces were held as shards by the panel frame. A few pieces had fallen onto the ledge of the window inside the living room. Grandpa cleaned the ledge first. He didn't see any glass on the carpet, but he vacuumed anyway to be on the safe side.

Then he went outside. A wide hedge stood in front of the window, but the hedge and house were far enough apart so that he could move between them. But he could not find even one piece of broken glass. He went so far as to use the wet vac to search the area and the hedge as best he could. Still, he found no glass. *This is becoming a major project*, he thought as he returned to the living room to pry the remaining shards from the frame.

A few minutes later, while he was carefully running his fingers around the inner surface of the empty frame to check his work, he looked outside and abruptly stopped feeling for glass. "What's that? That's odd," he whispered.

He couldn't put his head all the way through the frame, but he peered downward as best he could and saw something extraordinary. At first he couldn't clearly make it out. At ground level, between the house and the hedge, he saw what appeared to be the far side of a well-structured opening with a stairway leading downward into the ground. He backed off, wondering what the heck it was that he was looking at.

Again he put as much of his head through the frame as possible. He clearly saw part of a stairway.

"How can this be?" he whispered. "Am I seeing things?" He backed off and opened the window. He bent outward and looked down and saw the ground. There was nothing resembling a stairway. *Okay*, he thought, *I'm just nuts, huh?* Then he closed the window and again peered out through the empty frame. And again he clearly saw the far side of a stairway. This time he carefully looked around and saw a few pieces of broken glass near the stairway. He went outside and tapped the ground where the stairway should be. It was solid ground, and there was no glass lying around. He glanced around in a quandary and then returned to the living room—to think.

◊

"Hi Exi, Chel. Good to see you two." Grandpa greeted the girls with more brio than usual. He had a plan. "Which one of you has the smaller head? That would be the younger. Chel, come with me to the living room. All of you come. If I'm crazy, all of you will find out anyway."

Grandma asked, "What's all this about?" Grandpa had not yet informed her of his mysterious sighting.

"I don't know yet," Grandpa replied as they trailed into the living room.

"Girls, I accidentally broke a windowpane—here, in the lower half of the center window. The rope toy sailed through it. I've already discarded all of the broken glass I could find, and I checked several times to make sure there's no glass on the edges of the frame. Grandma, would you double check the frame for glass please?"

"But I couldn't find any glass outside. Now Chel, when Grandma is finished, I'm going to lift you up, and I want you to put your head through the empty frame and look down. Okay, here we go. What do you see?"

"I see a stairway going down into the ground. Never saw that before."

"Okay, let's come back inside." Grandpa then opened the window. "Now lean out and look down at the same place. What do you see?"

"Nothing, Grandpa, just ground between the hedge and the house. Hey, what neat magic, Grandpa!"

"I'm afraid not. Not mine, anyway," Grandpa admitted.

"So what's going on?" Grandma asked.

"I don't know," Grandpa answered, closing the window. "But whatever this is, it defies science as we know it."

He reflected on this for a moment, then turned and said that he was going to the garage and would be right back. He returned with a rounded hanging bell about the size of a baseball.

"What's that for?" Exi queried.

"Just want to see what happens if I put it through the empty frame and drop it. A little experiment. Exi, Chel, you two go outside and stand near the spot where the stairs are supposed to be. We'll call you back in after we drop the bell and ask you what you saw."

Grandma and Grandpa heard the bell bouncing down some concrete steps, and land. Grandpa listened carefully. "Yeah. It bounced down. Sounds deep. Fifty feet, I'd say."

Grandma reacted quickly. "Ooh, where does it go?"

They tried to understand this in terms of real-world ways but soon realized it would require some extrasensory investigation. Grandpa opened the window and called, "Come in, girls."

"No, we saw nothing. Nothing came out the window, nothing went through the ground."

But all this activity surrounding the bell reminded Exi of something else. "Where's the rope toy, Grandpa?"

"What a good question! It has to be in the yard." Looking out through the empty frame, Grandpa pointed to it. "There it is. Would you run out again, please, and get it?"

Exi ran out through the front door to the area where the rope toy should have been and looked all around, but it wasn't there. Grandpa again looked out through the glassless frame and saw it. Then he raised the window, and did *not* see it. Then he peered through a frame that contained a glass pane and did not see it. This pattern of seeing the rope toy was the same as that of seeing the stairway. The rope toy and the stairway were visible only though the glassless frame, not through normal processes.

Chel had a revelation. "That's why you didn't find the glass outside, Grandpa. Anything that goes through that empty frame, including the broken glass, goes into this … new world. Some of the glass probably fell down the stairway, and some may be scattered around it … in this new world."

Grandpa paused, "I like that description, Chel. It's like there are two worlds: the one we see outside while looking through the empty frame: and the one we see otherwise. While you two were outside, Grandma and I were discussing this. We think we're onto something revolutionary."

Grandma, who placed safety first in any venture, said, "It's important that we make a good, solid plan to explore this and that we find out as much as we can without putting ourselves in any danger. I was hesitant at first, but this is too important. At some point we may have to report this to authorities, whoever they may be."

Exi and Chel agreed. Chel volunteered herself. "If you take out some more panes, I could slip through and go down …"

"Absolutely not!" Grandma's outcry caused both girls to jump back from the window. "You two are not to go near this window! We love you too much. You can be part of this exploration at ground level. After Grandpa and I do some planning, we'll be ready for some kind of look-see first thing in the morning. Okay? In the meantime, let's not mention this to anyone except Molly until we find out more about it. She should be back soon from her telescope gazing project, and we'll explain what's going on. Her insight should be useful. Meanwhile, the living room is sealed off till we all can be here tomorrow."

$$\Diamond$$

"Good morning, girls," Grandma said to Exi and Chel amidst good morning hugs as they entered the house.

Molly, who had just finished breakfast, was in the living room with Grandpa near the broken window, holding Sparkles. "This is really something!" she said to the girls.

Earlier, Grandpa had removed the remaining seven windowpanes and their wood frames from the lower half of the center window, creating a space large enough for a person to slide through.

"So now the window is closed, but there's no glass in it," Grandma said. "You three may look through, but Grandpa and I will be holding onto you for safety. We have only two flashlights. Share."

"Wow!" They exclaimed in unison. "What a sight!" Exi declared.

"The stairway is so steep! Almost like a fancy ladder," Molly said. "And it seems to lead to a doorway to … under the house."

Grandpa asked the girls to step back. "Okay, now open this glassless window and look down."

The girls did so and saw only the ground.

"Yep," Grandpa said. "If you open the window or go outside for a look, it's just not there. But through the closed window with no glass, there it is. So is it, isn't it, or both?"

"Well, what's the answer?" Chel asked.

Grandpa said, "It looks like both places exist. But that would mean that both exist at the same place. We need to investigate this more."

"How do we do that?" Exi asked.

"The only way that Grandma and I can think of is for me to go down to see what's there—to open the door and peek in, using a flashlight if necessary. Exi, you and Chel go outside to witness all that occurs. One of you should stand in the yard facing the hedge and the window. The other should stand between the hedge and house, facing the spot under the window where the stairway would be, but about ten feet away from it.

"Okay? Grandma and Molly will witness things from inside the house, looking through the glassless window. The stairwell is deep, so Grandma and I will be in touch with our cell phones instead of yelling."

◊

Exi, facing the house, saw Grandpa approach the closed, glassless window. She saw him put one leg through the space where the glass panels had been, but as he inserted the leg to the outside, she saw it disappear or become invisible. The same happened with the other leg, and it happened with all of him as he slid himself out through the window.

And Chel, who had the side view, saw nothing exit through the window.

Inside, Grandma and Molly saw all of him climb out of the closed glassless window and climb down the stairs. With the help of a flashlight, they saw him standing on the small landing at the foot of the stairway, shoving the bell and the glass fragments to the side. They saw him look up and wave.

They waved back, and Grandma called him on her phone. "The phones work," he answered. Now they both knew that whatever it was they were experiencing, the seeming two worlds were not so disconnected that the phones wouldn't work. Not yet, anyway.

"Okay, here goes," Grandpa said.

"Wait!" shouted Grandma, looking down at him, forgetting that they were linked by phone. "Let me call Exi and Chel." She looked up to call them indoors so they could witness these proceedings. But they were not there! "Oh my God, where'd they go?" She was sure they wouldn't just run off.

Then she had a brilliant idea. She opened the window. There they were, in place like two good researchers. "Found you. Come on in and watch. He's going to peek in."

The four watched Grandpa carefully push the door ajar while extending the flashlight inside and aiming it in various directions.

"It's a dark place. It seems like a boring little room with nothing in it." At that, feeling as if he had been powerfully shoved, he found himself inside the room. The door closed behind him.

"Wait, don't!" Grandma quickly yelled through her phone. But by then it was too late.

His phone died. His flashlight fell to the floor, and there was no light. He felt an odd sensation, the likes of which he'd never experienced: a certain intense spinning sensation, a strange dizziness. He wanted to open the door and scramble out, but he was too disoriented for that. Then his "dead" phone rang. "Thank God," he muttered. He felt for the talk button. "Hi, sweetheart," he answered.

But a deep, haunting voice responded. "I am not your sweetheart. But let me say right up front that I am talking to your wife and grandchildren as we speak, assuring them in no uncertain terms that you are fine, and that you will remain fine."

"Who are you? Where am I?" Grandpa asked fearfully.

"You are fortunate. You're on a journey. A mission. Your objective is to save your own life."

Grandpa was speeding into a state of anxiety and felt faint. "Are you God?"

"We won't need the phone." The phone became disconnected, but the voice continued. "I called on that to lessen the shock you would've experienced by suddenly hearing a voice so nearby in a strange, dark place. You will be back with your loved ones in thirty minutes. You're traveling back in time and through space. You're going back many years. When you arrive at the destination, you will know what to do."

"I'm going back in time?" Grandpa asked.

"Yes, the past is one of the three components of time. But you don't know the other two components, do you? You need to."

Grandpa felt himself on the verge of unconsciousness. Time travel creates amazing sensations. You have the feeling of having no body, of floating. Darkness and vague images surround you. There is a pleasant mystical aspect to it. You become profoundly connected with your spiritual qualities, and less of the physical. The fear that Grandpa initially experienced faded away.

"Yes I do," Grandpa answered. "They're the past, the present, and the future."

"Nope. It's very important in your circumstances to understand some things about time. Not everything about time is so vastly complex. But a few things are."

"What do you mean by 'complex?'" Grandpa asked, now feeling more engaged by this conversation.

"I'll give you just one example. If you had an identical twin who, shortly after birth, moved to a massive heavenly body—much more massive than Earth—then your twin's timepiece would run slower than yours. Today your twin would be younger than you. Time is related to mass, acceleration, and energy.

"You just need to understand the three components of time if you want to know who I am. But it's not the past, present, and future, because there really is no present. The future continuously becomes the past. That is, the present is infinitesimally small. Its span is zero units of time. Philosophers, in the study of time, call this the 'philosophy of becoming.' St. Augustine wrote of the 'eternal now.' More informally, it has been referred to as the 'knife's edge,' continuously separating the past from the future.

"We use terms such as 'present,' 'presently,' 'now,' 'instant,' and such all the time because it's a convenience for communication. Do you understand what I'm talking about?"

"Well … maybe … sort of," Grandpa replied. "But then what are the three components of time?"

The voice answered, "They are the past, the future, and the *future* future."

"The future future? What pray tell is that?"

"I'll answer that as it pertains to a person—you, for example. You have a past. And you are going to visit the you of your past for a few seconds. You have a future. And when your future is finished, you will be in your *future* future. Know what I mean?"

"Yeah, I think so! That's after I die. The time I'm in after I die, right?"

"Right. Now you're in a position to know who I am. And no, I'm not God."

"Well?"

"I am you, visiting you from your future future!"

"Of course you wouldn't know me or anything else in the future future, except under unusually special circumstances such as what you are now experiencing. But you'll see one day that you are me. We're the same."

Grandpa rubbed his chin pensively. He mulled over what the voice was telling him and sensed that all he had heard was the truth, albeit he was far from comprehending it.

The voice continued, "I've come from your future future, and I am ushering you to a few seconds of time in your past in order for you to save your life. This doesn't involve anything physically dramatic such as a pending accident, rather something more psychiatric. I would do it myself if I could, but I'm almost totally invisible, and this job requires visibility."

Grandpa's future future continued to talk about this "new world" (as Chel had put it) as seen through the magic window. "This new world is simply a small part of the greater place where spirits reside. Occasionally, some of us will come back to this branch of the spirit world that shares space with Earth in order to accomplish some important task on Earth. We cannot judge the tasks. They are given to us to do. And we can't directly enter your world. We can't come back to spy on relatives, for example, but we can take a quick peek beyond the veil, if that's needed to accomplish the task. But if necessary, we can get an Earth-living human to enter our world temporarily—not the greater part, but the part that coexists in space with the human world—as I did with you.

"And when the task is accomplished and you are safely back home, we can erase all evidence of the spirit world. For example, there will be no stairway in the ground at the front of your house.

"But I can't remove the spirits' front yard until you remove something from it when you return, something that belongs in the human world. You will recognize it. Oh, and for the same reason, here's a pouch for the broken glass at the landing of the stairwell and on the ground near its opening. Small things like dust from your clothes don't matter. We just won't take anything larger than that, or anything of any possible value to humans.

"I won't see you again. When your task is completed, just take Molly and step back into the closet and sit on the floor ..."

"What? What do you mean, *Molly*?" Grandpa exclaimed. "And what *closet*?"

"When you entered the time tunnel, she rushed down the stairway, thinking maybe she could assist you by using some of her special abilities—knowledge about different worlds and such. And she will. She is a few seconds behind us, with her grandfather who lived on Friend until he went to the future future."

"Oh, wow!" Grandpa exclaimed.

"She and you will be fine. Listen, you'll find that she will be essential in your lifesaving mission. Now continue to enjoy the pleasures of time travel."

Grandpa instinctively felt this to be sincere and smiled. "Molly! What a special person."

Then the voice ceased, and Grandpa sensed that his time traveling was nearing an end. In his dreamlike state, he was still smiling. All of this time travel had been an overwhelming and awakening experience.

Finally, Grandpa found himself sitting on a closet floor, no longer traveling back in time. The closet light was on. He saw his arms and legs as faint abstractions of the actual—not invisible, but semitransparent. And he sensed that he was weightless. After a moment's reflection, he recognized the clothes and toys in the closet. They were his when he was nine years old.

Suddenly, Molly materialized next to him, smiling. "Hi, Grandpa."

They nervously gazed at each other as two people may do before opening a door to the unknown. "Thank you for joining me, Molly."

◊

Grandpa stood up and reached for the doorknob, but his weightlessness would not allow him to grip it. Instead, he simply passed through the door into his old bedroom, followed by Molly.

Molly stood in a corner next to the boy's small desk as Grandpa ambled up to the bed. The boy in the bed was having a nightmare and crying. Suddenly he awoke to see a faintly visible senior citizen standing at the foot of his bed. He stopped crying and was silent for a moment. "Are you my future? Are you my future?" he asked.

The senior answered, "Yes, Roger, I am your future." Then something caught young Roger's eye. He looked through the shadows created by the full moon and the bathroom light, toward the corner near his small desk. He raised his head off the pillow, rubbed his eyes, blinked a few times, stared for a few seconds, acquired a huge smile, and then fell into the soundest sleep he had ever had.

Grandpa went up to the boy's head to stroke it once and blew him a kiss. Turning toward Molly, he pointed to the closet. Sitting on the closet floor, Molly expressed her mystification. "What in the world was that all about? My other grandfather told me you were supposed to save his life."

"I did, and you did too, Molly. Mainly you! We saved him from an awful death. Now I understand something that I've wondered about all my life. I'll explain all this to you and the others when we return ... when we return."

During the brief phase forward in time, Grandpa added, "Then you will know yourself better, Molly." Soon the back of the closet opened like door, and they saw the stairway. Grandpa noticed that he was holding his flashlight, which now cast light. And he had his cell phone, which now worked.

When they were on the landing, the door closed behind them. There they witnessed the door convert to a vertical layer of dirt. The world of the future future was changing back into the world of pasts and futures—the human world. They picked up the few pieces of glass and the bell, put them in the pouch, and climbed up the stairway.

When they reached ground level, they stood by the hedge and looked down, and noted that the stairway had disappeared behind them. Ground was there as usual—the original worldly ground. Then they picked up the nearby remaining glass around the hedge, and that area too, was now back as part of the original usual world.

Grandpa said to Molly, "Thank you for your company and support. You made all the difference in the world." Then they crawled into the house through the closed, glassless window.

$$\Diamond$$

"Grandma, girls, let's sit down here in the living room. I have something to tell you that I've never mentioned to anyone."

Grandma interjected, "Let me bring some coffee and stuff. This promises to be an interesting exchange. But first, it's good to see you. That voice on the phone convinced us that you'd be okay."

When they all got comfortable, Grandpa began. "When I was a boy, just nine years old, I developed a phobia. It's called *thanatophobia*."

"What?" Exi asked. "What the heck is that?"

"That's what I want to explain. First of all, a certain amount of fear of dying or fear of death is natural and healthy. It helps to keep us alive. It's part of our fight-or-flight nature. It's normal, like pain. We don't like pain, but if we couldn't feel it, we would not do well in recognizing and avoiding serious dangers. But an excessive amount of this fear of death—an amount qualifying as a phobia—is called thanatophobia. Unless treated, it can harm the quality of life, even shorten it.

"When I was nine years old, I developed a serious case of this phobia. I was certain I was going to die soon, and I was very much in fear of that. Then I realized that I was going to die of this fear. I was going to die from being so overpoweringly afraid of dying. I couldn't eat. This fear was now the essence of me. I was crazy. My parents and various doctors tried everything they could think of.

"Then one night, while having one of my nightmares, I sensed a presence in my room. I suddenly woke up to see standing at the foot of my bed, in a semitransparent form, a kindly looking and healthy man. I remember thinking that other than age he kind of resembled me. I was not frightened and sensed something positive. I distinctively remember asking him, 'Are you my future? Are you my future?' and I'll never forget his assertive answer: 'Yes, Roger, I am your future.'

"Then … something special caught my eye, a mystical happening. I looked toward a corner of my room near my desk, and I saw this beautiful angel. I mean … it's hard to describe. She was semitransparent and slightly wavering, so I couldn't get a perfect look, but I felt a profound beauty, and I sensed a deep caring for me and love. She was smiling at me. Her wings rose in the air, and she brightened with colors. She waved. I sensed she was going to float toward me. This was truly something special. A certain inner strength radiated from her to me, and it forever became a part of me. I knew then that I had a guardian angel.

"I fell into the most restful sleep, and my phobia vanished forever."

Molly was speechless, and her eyes swelled with tears.

Grandpa smiled at Molly. "Now, after all these years, I learned that it was you in that corner, Molly." His smile continued, even while choking on his tears.

$\Diamond$

Grandma stepped over to Molly and put her arms on her shoulders. "So this morning you and Grandpa went back in time—or some spiritual part of you did—and completed that circle? That reassuring, hypnotic, voice told us that you two were on a time trip to the past."

"Completing the circle—that's a good way of putting it," Grandpa said. "Yes, it had to be, or else my recovery from this phobia would never have happened, and I would not be here today. But it was a marvelous and extraordinarily enlightening trip. Time travel is absolutely sensational, isn't it Molly?"

Molly nodded in agreement, still overwhelmed by the emotions swelling within her and trying to unravel the circumstances of Grandpa's childhood transformation in which she had mysteriously played a role.

The family knew that Grandma's thoughts often lead to insights into deep mysteries. She reflected that here. "And not only would Grandpa not be here, nether would our grandchildren. And maybe Molly would never have been discovered here on Earth by two friends who weren't frightened by her, helped shield her, and helped her appearance to become human through a developing friendship. At least she avoided a sad misadventure, such as being otherwise discovered and placed in some institution."

Grandma felt the moments of silence that followed, and then she qualified her remarks. "Maybe."

Again, Grandpa smiled at Molly. "You didn't know you were here on Earth over half a century ago, eh?"

Molly smiled back. "No. It baffles me. There is so much to think about here. I don't recall discussions of time travel among the friendlings, but in thinking of their long travels in terms of light years, I now wonder if time travel played a role. But you're right, Grandpa. I went back in time farther than my age on this trip. I could have even taken three-year-old Sparkles with me back to your childhood. Think about that."

Chel began looking around on the floor and on the sofas. She stood up for a better view of the room. Then she had to ask, "Where is Sparkles?"

They all dashed to the window. And there he was, in the front yard, the remaining part of the new world, playing with his rope toy. "Oh, yeah!" Grandpa quipped, before making a second trip through the glassless window—no, not the open window—to bring puppy and toy back inside the same way. As they crawled back through the window, the window returned to normal, with wood frames and glass panes. The shared occupancy with the world of the future future (as the future Roger had put it) was gone from Earth. The world was one again.

"Back to normal now!" Grandpa exclaimed. "All is back to normal." He pondered the word *normal*. "You know, there are some inseparable and complex issues at play here: time, space, angels, and ... hidden dimensions. We'll be talking about these things for months. For *years*." He stepped over to Molly. "But first things first. Thank you, angel." He put his arms around her. "Thank you for saving my life."

L-Shaped Time

"Other worlds ... real magic ... way-out beings ... whatever." Exi was once again relaxing with Chel at the beach. "Are these real happenings, or what? Anyway, it's always good to be back here on good old planet Earth, right?"

Chel, lying back and viewing the sun-swept ocean, nodded in agreement. "Yup. You know, it wasn't that long ago when we first met Molly. And we weren't far from here on the beach when we received that crazy call. Remember all that?"

This time they were vacationing at their new beach house. It was their first stay at the house since their brief visit to verify that this gift really existed. Grandpa and Grandma called it the Molly House, for it was Molly who successfully battled the foremost source of evil lurking among the amronians.

This morning's bask at the beach was at the top of their list for the family vacation, which began late the day before when Grandpa, Grandma, Exi, and Chel arrived at the Molly House. Molly was to arrive in two days, after completing a course at the state university on, of all topics, time, space, and energy. (She was the only adolescent in that graduate school physics class.)

For a while in the afternoon, after their beach visit, Exi and Chel helped Grandpa with some chores before he left to host a magic show at a nearby town, but he also planned to return in two days.

Then all would be there for Carl's first visit to Earth. He planned to conduct a space-time journey from Amron, and to join the family after everyone finally settled in at his gift of appreciation, the Molly House.

◊

The next day also began with fun. Exi and Chel woke up happy-spirited, without a clue that a mysterious event was in the works. It began as they were walking down the two-hundred-yard road entering their neighborhood after a morning of roaming through some nearby beach shops.

The neighborhood pond captured their view to the left, and a row of beach houses bordering the road was on their right. They looked slightly to the left at the Molly House across part of the pond, a picturesque view while strolling down the entrance road.

"Look, Exi!" Chel said, stopping to point at Grandpa's van in the driveway. "Grandpa's back."

"Oh yeah, I see. But he wasn't supposed to be back here till tomorrow. I wonder what's going on."

They continued walking down the narrow road, viewing the pond and yards. As usual, their view to the left was obstructed by a thick grove of tall shrubs as they neared the left turn that again skirts the pond and leads to the Molly House a few houses down.

As they passed the shrubs and turned for the shorter walk to the house, Exi nudged Chel. They slowed down and focused on the driveway. "The van's gone," Exi uttered.

"So? That's no big deal," Chel said. "Maybe he left and went the other way … Oh, but it dead-ends at the canal. He would have come our way."

"Or he pulled into someone else's driveway," Exi speculated. "Anyway, we'll find out from Grandma in a minute."

Grandma laughed. "Girls, he left yesterday for the show once we settled in. And no, he hasn't been here. I spoke with him just an hour ago. He'll be back tomorrow. I'll make arrangements for you two to get your eyes tested."

The two did not think that was funny. They strolled through the back door for the beach.

"What's going on?" Exi asked.

"Don't know. We saw the van, right?"

"Yes, both of us. We've gotta figure this out. Okay, first we went down the entrance and we saw the van in the driveway, right? Then we turned just past the shrubs, and it was gone."

"It's like it just vanished when we made the turn," Chel said.

"But we can agree on two things," Exi said. "We both saw Grandpa's van, yet we know Grandma tells the truth. It wasn't there. So go figure. What causes such a paradox?"

A paradox, once recognized as such, tends to silence people for a while. They walked onto the nearby pier and watched the rising mounds of ocean rolling past, and swelling into waves before pounding the shore. They sat on a bench facing the peaceful view. Finally, Exi came forth with a bold notion.

"Chel, the only explanation that I can think of is this. As we came down the first leg, we saw the van as it was yesterday, before he left for the show—backed in because he brought home the new beach chairs for us to help unload. Then as we turned the corner, we saw the driveway as it is today—empty."

"You're saying we saw into the past while on the first road?"

They became silent and motionless on the bench and gazed out into the ocean.

Finally Chel continued. "Seems like it's the only explanation that fits, except … isn't that impossible? I mean, people in the here and now can't really watch nearby things happening in the past, unless it's on a film or something."

"I wish Molly were here," Exi muttered. She would have some ideas. But she'll be here tomorrow, before Grandpa. Oh, and Carl will be here the day after tomorrow. If anyone could understand this, it'd be Carl."

"Yeah … well Molly should know something too," Chel responded. "Today is her exam in that advanced whatever science course."

"Advanced space-time physics," Exi said, standing up. "Let's go back to the entrance and look into the past again."

◊

"There's the van again," Chel said, pointing.

"Yep!" Exi exclaimed. "And now the trunk is opened."

"Wait, look!" Chel screamed.

They stopped to see Grandpa and themselves walk out of the house, remove some chairs from the van, and carry them around to the back of the house.

"Move it," Chel shouted. The two ran to the end of that first leg and turned left just past the shrubs. The driveway was empty.

"That proves it!" Exi announced triumphantly.

When they reached the driveway, they turned back to face the entrance road just beyond the pond. They were deep in thought.

"Why can't this work both ways?" Exi asked. "If you see into the past when you look from up there to here, why can't you see the past looking from here to up there too? Maybe we can and just don't know it yet. We should do an experiment."

"Or into the future!" Chel interjected. "If we see into the past by looking from there to here, maybe we can see into the future by looking from here to there."

Then came the shocker. Across the way they saw a figure turning into the neighborhood at the far end of the entrance road.

"Oh wow!" Chel cried out. "She's not supposed to be here till tomorrow!"

"Well guess what, Chel, I bet you're right. We are looking into the future—twenty-four hours into the future." Then they waved heartily to Molly, and Molly waved back.

"Wait," Exi cried out. "How can that be?"

"We're looking a day into the future and she's looking a day into the past, so doesn't that make sense? Wouldn't we see one another?"

"Yeah ... I guess?"

$$\Diamond$$

The roads throughout the neighborhood were not through streets, and they were narrow. Traffic was sparse, and the roads were used for walking as well as for driving. Exi and Chel were peacefully watching

Molly progress down the road when they suddenly screamed in fear. They witnessed a car backing quickly out of a driveway, leveled for Molly. Molly didn't see the car in time. When it was upon her, she instinctively reached out with her right arm and scrambled to her left, but it was too late. The car's hefty trunk met her hip and ribcage. She tumbled down the steep twenty-foot embankment toward the pond and its brambles. Her fall ended when her head smacked a boulder, and she bounced face-first into the water. She remained there, motionless, and the old gray sedan slowly pulled out of the neighborhood as if nothing had happened.

"Oh my God, we gotta get there!" Exi yelled as she and Chel began running down the road. When they reached the shrubs, they turned right and ran to where the car hit Molly, then scrambled down the bank and searched. But Molly was not to be seen. Exi grasped the strange reality. "We are reacting today, but all this happens tomorrow, as we saw from the driveway, looking into the future!"

On her hands and knees in the water, Chel screamed, "Oh, oh, oh God!" Then she reached for the rocky edge and looked up. "We've gotta stop it!"

On their way back to the Molly House, Exi raised the essential point: "Can we alter the future once we've seen what's already there? Is that possible?"

Chel wouldn't philosophize about it. "We've gotta do something!"

The girls guessed when Molly would be finished with her exam and tried to call her several times, but her phone was off. They figured that she turned it off for her exam and had not yet thought to turn it back on. So they left an unnerving message about her immediate future disaster with the car, which they later wished they hadn't done.

Chel looked at Exi. "Now what?"

"Don't know. No one's going to believe this. We need to think and do something."

They sat comfortably on the backyard porch, and gazed out over the calm gray ocean, anxiously looking for answers.

Exi broke the silence. "I wonder if you can really change the future. I mean, it seems like the future that we saw here must be the future that happens, right?"

"I just don't know. But if we actually see the future, and then change one of the things leading up to it, then won't we change the future? For example, if we were to dynamite the car, then it couldn't run into Molly."

"I sure hope it couldn't. We won't do exactly that." Exi paused. "We'll soon find out if we can alter the future by altering something here and now. That's the only way I can think of to save Molly from this horrible …" She lowered her head.

$$\Diamond$$

After much thought, they conceived three plans for saving Molly. The first was a direct interference. They would meet Molly as she entered the neighborhood, stop her, talk with her about her impending fate, or, by some other way, delay her for a few minutes. But they figured that since Molly did not return their call, she may have been wondering about their strange message and may react oddly. At any rate, they felt uneasy about direct interaction with her at the last minute and deemed this plan as an alternative.

The second plan was to release the air from all four tires of the gray sedan shortly before the driver climbs in to back out. But they could get caught, or Molly could get blamed for it, or a number of other negative consequences could happen. This too would be held as an alternative.

The third plan was to be activated in the morning, after finding out some things about the people living at the house with the gray sedan. If this plan didn't work, there would be time to deploy the others. Having a sequence of plans is a sound strategy where a life is at stake. The sisters demonstrated their keen insight.

Early that evening Exi and Chel walked to the house next door to the one with the gray sedan.

"Hello," the boy who lived there said while opening the door.

"Hi," Exi said. "You're Bob, aren't you?"

"Yes," Bob said, nodding.

"I'm Exi, and this is my sister Chel. We just …"

"Oh yeah, come on in," Bob said, backing up and holding the door open. "I've seen you. You all are vacationing over there on the beach."

Exi and Chel met Bob's parents, and all five chatted for a few minutes. When the small talk slowed, Bob responded to his intuition. "I sense you two want to ask me about something, right?"

"Yes," Chel said.

"Okay, let's go to the porch." Bob led the way.

Exi and Chel sat next to each other on the comfortable love seat, and Bob sat facing them on a patio chair. Exi began. "This is a little embarrassing because we need to know a little about someone we think you know, but we can't tell you why yet. Maybe in a day or so."

"Sure," Bob said. "Who are we talking about?"

"Your next-door neighbors with the old gray sedan," Exi answered. "Who drives the sedan? What's he or she like? What does he or she do?"

"Only one person lives there, a man, maybe in his sixties: Mr. Anderson. I don't know his first name. He's kind of moody, I'd say, and he doesn't talk much. I think he's retired but works part time as a baggage checker at the airport. I'm not sure what his work schedule is, but he leaves his house late in the afternoons. What else would you like to know?"

"Do you have his telephone number?" Chel asked. "We want to talk with him, although from what you said, it sounds like it won't be fun." Bob copied the number from the community directory as his mother came in and left a tray of cookies and a pitcher of iced tea. The three merrily chatted for a while, and then Bob walked the girls home.

Once inside their house, the two had a big smile for each another.

"What a nice guy," Chel said while Exi was still smiling. "And did you see the way he was looking at you, Exi?"

"Oh, Chel ..."

But their smiles waned as the urgency of their mission returned.

◊

At nine thirty in the morning, Chel picked up the phone and dialed the number.

A dull voice answered, "Hello."

"Hello, Mr. Anderson. My name is Betty, and I've been asked to call all persons who plan on being at work at the airport today to remind them that we are on daylight saving time beginning today."

"Oh, wow! I didn't know."

"So you need to turn the hour hands of your time pieces forward an hour, understand?"

"Okay, I'll do that now."

"Thank you, Mr. Anderson. Have a good day. Bye now."

$$\Diamond$$

In the early afternoon, Grandma joined the girls in the driveway. "The beach, the pier, the backyard view, the shops ... and you two are just sitting in the driveway, looking at the street?"

Chel responded, "We're leaving in a little while, Grandma. We're doing a little experiment. We'll tell you about it later."

Grandma's quizzical expression remained as she stepped back inside.

A little more time of nothingness passed when Exi announced, "It's a quarter till three, time to go."

They snuggled in with the shrubs on the entrance road so they could keep a low lookout for any activity.

"Just a few minutes now!" Exi quietly exclaimed. "Oh—it's working! There he is now, getting in the car!"

The old gray sedan began backing out of the driveway at three o'clock—an hour earlier than usual—and crept out of the neighborhood with no incident.

The two hugged each other. "It worked!" Exi exclaimed. "At least so far."

Chel conveyed her thoughts. "Think about it. We've altered the future—the future that we saw yesterday—the future that would have happened. We sure did it! But how does all this really work?"

While waiting for Molly, Exi and Chel spent most of the time trying to sort out their experiences with time. Then at a few minutes before four, they began their walk up to the entrance.

"There she is!" Chel shouted. "Oh … and she's waving to us as we were yesterday, in the driveway. Ha, she could see us there yesterday and here today—at the same time."

"You can speculate later, Chel. Hustle!"

They hurried to greet her. She was lugging a suitcase and moving at a slower pace. They met between the sedan's driveway and the neighborhood entrance and exchanged greetings, whereupon Exi grabbed the suitcase, and the three began their trek to the Molly House.

When they passed the sedan's driveway, Exi loosened up and cheered. "You're safe now, Molly!"

Molly slowed down and said to Exi, "Safe? I have to know something. Are you talking about what you told me yesterday in your message? About a car backing out of a driveway and knocking me down the bank?"

Exi turned and pointed. "Yes! This driveway we just passed."

Molly shook her head. "Never happened. You just now saw that it never happened. I'm here—safely past the driveway."

"But it was supposed to have happened. Chel and I changed all that. We'll explain."

Chel said, "Molly, something else is different—something about time. During the time that we waved at each other yesterday … well, it was yesterday for us … you were looking into the past, and we were looking into the future."

Molly swayed to one side, then to the other. "Into the past … into the future. What's all this about? You have a lot of explaining to do."

Exi said, "You know about time travel. You even did that with Grandpa. Molly, Chel's right. From our telephone message yesterday, we figured you thought that looking into the past and into the future is impossible, but we want to show you that, at least on one place on Earth, we can look at another place and see future events happen, and if we go to the second place and look back to the first, we can see past events happen. We're going to prove it to you."

Molly was polite and only smiled. "This would be vastly different from the trip to the past I took with Grandpa. That was a miracle of a type that happens only once in a thousand years on one out of many planets." She paused for a for a few seconds of deep thought, and concluded with "Hmm."

"Okay, we're near the driveway" Chel said. "Just a few more steps ... Molly, turn around and face the entrance, and wave and jump. Or stand on you head. Do something strange." Chel checked the time. "Molly, tomorrow at four twenty we're going up there to look back here and see us doing all this today." Chel smiled at Molly. "You'll see yourself standing on your hands and waving with your feet!"

"Oh, Look," Exi said pointing. They saw Grandpa's van coming their way past the shrubs for the final stretch home.

Exi and Chel smiled when Molly placed a hand to her chin and faintly said, "That's weird, I didn't see him come down the entrance road while we were just now staring over there."

"That's because he's coming home today, not tomorrow," Exi tendered. "See?"

Molly didn't answer.

The three waved as Grandpa parked his van.

◊

If the sky around Earth could smile, it probably would have on the morning of the arrival of a being from another galaxy. Carl arrived at ten thirty. Grandma was being surrounded by Grandpa, Molly, Exi, Chel, and Sparkles as she opened the front door. Carl had to wear cleverly designed clothing in order to look human, which was not an easy task in sunny beach weather. But he did it well. He was completely wrapped in a large red, white, and blue beach towel, and he sported a large, white hat with a drooping brim, and large, dark-framed sunglasses. He bore no visible luggage. He wore shoes that added three inches to his height and were hidden by the long towel. Moreover, he was whirling a cane and whistling. Any earthling he may have encountered along the way to the Molly House would have viewed him as eccentric, but not as a monkey from outer space.

Carl stripped off his wraps as he stepped into the foyer, and everyone simultaneously exchanged greetings. But he had a special smiling hug for Molly. Sparkles stood on his hind feet and yipped, and

Carl reached down to say, "Ah, so you remember me, huh Sparkles? Good to see you, boy."

Grandma had prepared a festive brunch for this joyful reunion. She remembered Carl likes human foods. They continued chatting while ambling into the kitchen to begin a warm and interesting get-together. As they were sitting down, Grandma asked the question she had been wondering about every day: "Carl, how's everything on Amron?"

"Great! Just great since Molly obliterated the pervasive presence of Mr. Evil." He smiled again at Molly ... and Molly slightly blushed.

"That was my honor, Carl. I'm just glad I could do it."

So early on the conversation focused on happenings on Amron. Then Grandpa raised a key question. "How did you arrive here from so far in outer space, Carl? What's your mode of travel?"

"Good question, Roger. It's not by spaceships like you earthlings think of them. It does have much to do with space, but it has as much or more to do with time. I really can't answer the question completely without you having an extensive science background. We live in a galaxy that's so far away, that even if we travel at the speed of light—through space but not time—it would take millions of years to arrive on Earth. We have to travel through time as well to make it all happen."

That's all Exi and Chel needed to hear in order to broach their recent experience with Molly and time. Everyone listened attentively for Carl's response.

Carl registered surprise upon hearing about the sisters' experience. "That's extremely rare on Earth and elsewhere. You know what you did? The two of you experienced a five-dimensional, L-shaped, convoluted, bounded, time-cyclic, gravity-enfolded space warp—an *L-structure* for short."

"Whoa!" Molly replied. "I've been taking advanced physics courses, but I've never heard of anything like that.

"I know, I know. Sorry," Carl said. As you know, we amronians have been around for a long time, and we've reached advanced understandings about the foundations and extents of our cosmos and about what it contains. And we're still searching.

"Anyway, L-structures are invisible, intangible forms for engulfing various environments, such as these two roads. They are generally shaped like the letter *L*, but they can adjust to whatever shape is suitable for a special project.

"Scientists from Friend, Amron, and three other faraway planets have been collecting data about L-structures for many centuries, but we still know little about them or where they come from.

"They rarely occur—maybe once every few thousand years or so—on planets that are inhabited by intelligent life. They occur in certain essential matters involving the universe and its beings. The purpose of an L-structure involves, first, gaining the attention of a few inhabitants of the planet. These inhabitants will witness a heartbreaking event happen in the future, and then they'll focus on altering things in the present in order to prevent that sad future event from happening. Of course, sad events happen all the time. And planetary beings cannot predict them. In fact, they know that such future events don't yet exist, so they are not predictable. Yet, from a higher level, for incredibly special purposes ..."

"Wait, that's about us!" Chel impulsively interrupted.

"Yeah!" cried Exi. "And the special purpose was saving Molly!"

Everyone looked at Molly.

"Exactly," Carl responded.

Then curiously, he asked, "Now let me ask you something. You know, I've never seen an L-structure. Does the one here still exist?"

"Yes," Exi said. "Well ... we think so. Before four o'clock, we're planning to trek over to the entrance and look across the pond at the driveway to see the three of us turning the cartwheels and stuff that we did yesterday. This was to be proof to Molly that such views into the future and the past are possible. But by now I think she knows." Exi winked at Molly.

Molly winked back with a smile.

Carl noted this and smiled. He said, "This means that if you do see a tragedy happen in the future—knowing that you are indeed looking into the future—then you may be able to devise some adjustments in the present so that the future tragedy won't happen. But, if you cannot see into the future, then you can't foresee tragedy, and therefore can't avoid it."

He looked around at everyone. "Profound, huh?"

Silence.

◊

They continued chatting for a while before Carl closed his eyes to fathom the time, and then he looked up at Exi and Chel. "Like I said earlier, I've never seen an L-structure. Let's go to wherever you said and watch you three girls perform here in the driveway ... yesterday."

Grandpa stood and walked to the door to grab Sparkles's leash, whereupon Sparkles took the hint and bounded for the door. Meanwhile, Carl quickly put on his disguise. The group left the house, scurried to the far end of the entrance road, stepped off onto a clearing near the pond, and faced the driveway.

After a short wait, the show began. They watched yesterday's Exi, Chel, and Molly trek from the road onto the driveway and turn around to face the pond. Exi and Chel jumped up and down and turned cartwheels, while Molly conducted a set of her acrobatic stunts, including standing on her hands and waving with her feet. Then Molly rotated back to her feet and executed a high flip in the air. Exi and Chel stood, faced the audience across the pond, and pointed toward Molly.

Then the unexpected happened. As Molly was into her second jump, many feet in the air, and before she even began preparation for a landing, she completely vanished, along with Exi and Chel. Absolutely no sign of life was seen on the driveway. In their place was Grandpa's van. It was not yet in the driveway during the performance.

Grandma screamed first. "My God! What happened?"

Carl replied, "Hey, they're standing here with us. Remember we were just looking into the past over there. Yesterday."

"Yes!" Molly confirmed. "And now we're looking into the present over there. The van's there now. It seems like the past just suddenly disappeared."

◊

All, including Sparkles, were still focused on the driveway when a life-changing event began to unravel. A blinding light flashed above the center of the driveway. It lasted for a second, and it left an afterglow that began to slowly enlarge.

The glow sparkled. It began stirring around, bulging, and shriveling. It evolved into a long collection of colorful strands of an unrecognizable origin, twisted together in seemingly chaotic ways. This oddity then slightly rose with various twirling motions, and began moving toward the viewers like a slow-rolling, shuddering tumbleweed, leaving the driveway and stopping above the center of the road before reaching the pond.

"My God," cried Chel. "What is it?"

Fingers were now recognized—so bright and glittery! A huge hand extended outward. It was a right hand, and it began swaying from side to side.

"It's waving!" Carl declared. All shyly waved back.

"Some kind of mystical presence," Carl added. "Must be."

"Ooh!" Exi cried and stepped closer to Carl.

◊

A smaller bright left hand (still much larger than a human hand) emerged from the mysterious complex of chaotic twirls. It also waved before plunging—with no visible arms—down into the ground. The large right hand continued to face the onlookers.

The twirling abstraction was shrinking. The large hand was capturing the attention.

The tips of the forefinger and thumb of the hand met, forming a circle, while the other three fingers fanned out. It moved back and forth in front of the onlookers who took this to mean "all is okay."

An earsplitting crack filled the air.

"It snapped its fingers," Carl said, "probably to make sure we're all still looking over there—focusing our attention there." All were.

Carl continued: "Earlier we were looking over there, into yesterday, at all the cartwheels and dancing and stuff because the L-structure was operating. Now we're seeing things as they are today. The L-structure is no longer operating. The hands took care of all that. It all stopped while we were watching Molly in mid-air during her stunt."

The smaller left hand reappeared from under the ground and was gripping something that no one could clearly see. But they saw bright lights streaming out from between the fingers. Then the hand swiftly ascended into the sky and vanished.

A few seconds later it reappeared, holding nothing and waving.

"The L-structure must be gone now," Carl said.

"Look!" Molly pointed. "The two hands are beginning to change shape." Their brightness dimmed, and they became smaller, ultimately to the size of human hands, and they moved closer to each other.

Sparkles, who was lying down through all this yet looking across the pond, stood and began wagging his tail. He began making his familiar yearning sounds.

"What on Earth does Sparkles see that we don't?" Molly asked.

Sparkles began a friendly barking and swayed from side to side on his front paws, as the two hands floated above the pond.

Grandma whispered, "Oh, they're coming our way."

Grandpa reacted too. "We're safe here, don't you think, Carl?"

They felt that there was no danger. For one thing, they realized that the hands had just dismantled the L-structure.

As the hands drifted closer, the observers noticed a smoky substance surfacing from near where the wrists would be. The substance was becoming thicker as the hands continued to slowly flow in the air above the pond toward them. Halfway to them, the substance began solidifying.

Chel exclaimed, "Oh look—arms! Bare arms are growing out from each hand. Oh, and now shoulders dressed in pink sleeves are coming out of the arms!"

"Pink? ... No!" Grandpa exclaimed.

All became aware of a spiritual being. A beautiful gown twirled around and fanned out as she hovered above ground level. She offered a beautiful, smiling face, and she gracefully flowed closer with outstretched arms and opened hands.

All did see beauty, but what they observed varied somewhat among them. The variations mostly pertained to features of her face. Yet all were looking at the same being. As future conversations would reveal, Molly's view varied the most. While she, like the others, saw beauty in the elusive approaching presence, she sensed certain resemblances with the friendlings with whom she spent much of her early life. Of course the others would not see that. And their future conversations would be far-reaching.

Chel took a step forward. "Oh … I think I see … misty-like … No! They're huge white wings. Gorgeous!"

Celestial music from an unknown source filled the air, a heavenly creation of mystifying and engaging blends of echoing tones.

The angel came to a rest in front of Sparkles, who was standing on his hind legs and instinctively stretching for a hug. She faced him, and after an engaging hug, Sparkles displayed a stunning smile and continued gazing at the wondrous beauty.

A few seconds of silence passed as the angel smiled and waved at Grandma, Grandpa, and Carl. Then she turned to Molly and placed her hands on Molly's cheeks. Her eyes said it all. She beheld Molly's eyes for a full minute as Molly sensed a certain love and a strong feeling of appreciation—and a sequence of unspoken messages that would unravel over the years.

And then she moved over to Exi and Chel and took them both into her arms, giving each a kiss on their foreheads. She did not speak from her smiling face. Her message was mental. "Bless you two who saved Molly. I represent many. We offer our praises."

Then she drifted back over the water, still facing the others. Her spreading wings and her larger-than-life bright radiance of love presented a mystical testimony for celestial existences somewhere within or beyond human notions of the cosmos. Then she disappeared with a smile, leaving only a voice in the air: "I'll be back."

◊

The walk back to the Molly House began in silence, with some twists and upward looks to see what may.

"Let's settle on the backyard porch and discuss all this," Grandpa said. Grandma added, "I'll bring out some snacks."

When they became comfortably seated around the porch table, Carl shared the clear but deep truth: "Molly is beloved by much higher forms of life."

Then he showed a side of himself that no one here had yet seen. Tears came to his eyes. Turning to Molly, he said, "That much beloved!" He continued revering her with a tender smile. "Yes, it's clear."

But Molly had to change the direction of the conversation. "I should not be the center of attention here. My word ... Exi and Chel saved my life! *That's* the accomplishment!"

"Molly's right," Carl agreed. "Exi and Chel certainly deserve our highest admiration for all that. And Molly knows better than any of us about the help and support that they provided in her encounters with other life and the wonders of our universe.

Carl paused and quickly fathomed Molly's history. "Yes, Exi and Chel saved her life. But remember also: they helped her to begin her life here as an earthling—as Mollyboltrightstagrut. Remember all that? It was a new beginning!"

All remembered. But the miracle of the angelic happening was not yet over.

Small, colorfully bow-tied packages materialized right in front of Exi, Chel, and Molly. Each quietly opened her gift.

The L-shaped charms glowed and sparkled more brilliantly than anything anyone on Earth had ever seen. Their beauty was breathtaking. Each was comprised of a blend of curious celestial items that would wow the world. Their radiances came from a far, far, faraway star.

As they admired their gifts, they began to notice an inviting curiosity. The jeweled details suggested shapes of keys. When the three noticed this, they looked up at each other in awe before looking down again. Then each saw another gift mysteriously appear in her other hand: a brightly colored, star-decorated, sealed envelope. What a day! What a future!

Printed in the United States
By Bookmasters